Frontier Man

FRONTIER MAN

BY Bonnie J. Flessen

RESOURCE *Publications* · Eugene, Oregon

FRONTIER MAN

Resource Publications
An Imprint of Wipf and Stock Publishers
199 W. 8th Ave., Suite 3
Eugene, OR 97401

www.wipfandstock.com

PAPERBACK ISBN: 979-8-3852-3915-3
HARDCOVER ISBN: 979-8-3852-3916-0
EBOOK ISBN: 979-8-3852-3917-7

VERSION NUMBER 01/22/25

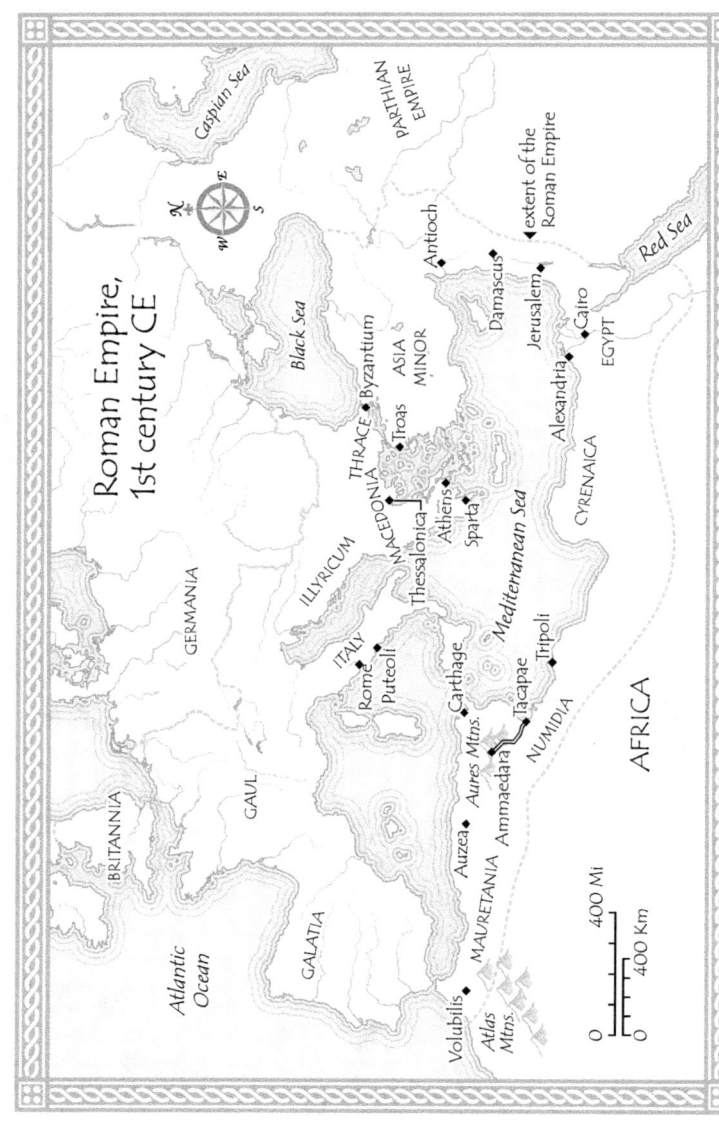

Roman Empire, 1st century CE

Atlantic Ocean
BRITANNIA
GALATIA
GERMANIA
GAUL
ITALY
Rome
Puteoli
Volubilis
Atlas Mtns.
MAURETANIA
Auzea
Aures Mtns.
Ammaedara
Tacapae
Carthage
Tripoli
NUMIDIA
AFRICA
Mediterranean Sea
ILLYRICUM
MACEDONIA
Thessalonica
Athens
Sparta
THRACE
Byzantium
Troas
ASIA MINOR
Black Sea
Caspian Sea
PARTHIAN EMPIRE
Antioch
Damascus
Jerusalem
Cairo
EGYPT
Alexandria
CYRENAICA
Red Sea
extent of the Roman Empire

N
S
E
W

0   400 Mi
0   400 Km

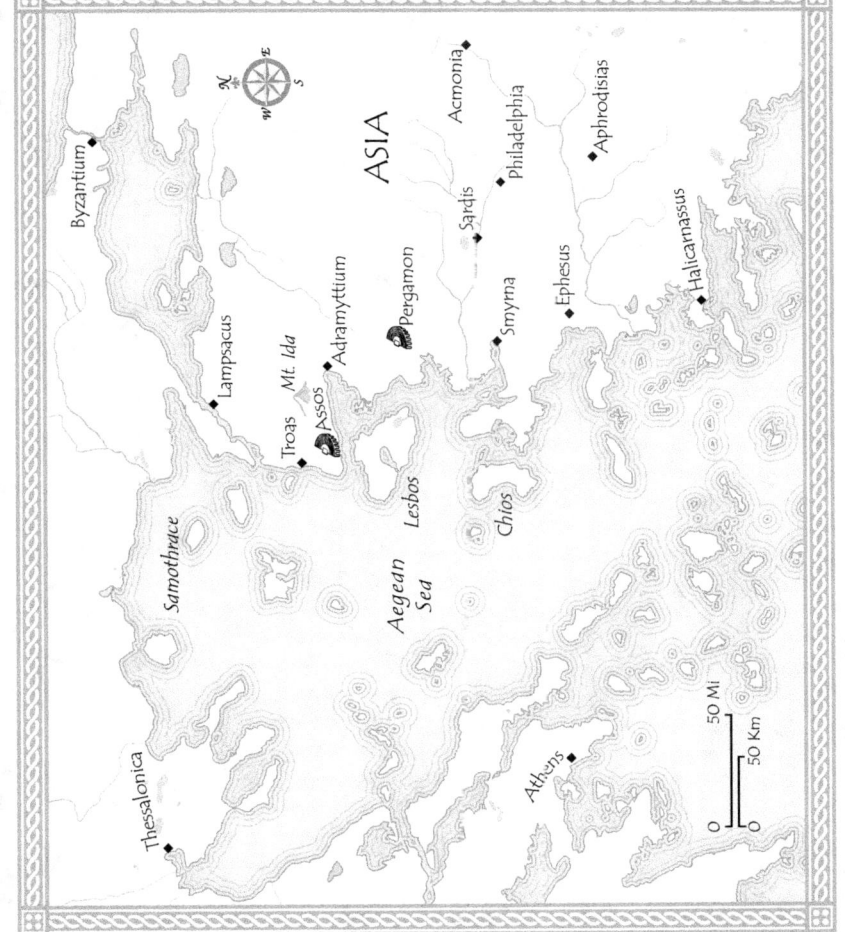

List of Characters

Domitia, later known as **Kaineus:** Wealthy widow from Pergamum. Member of an elite family of political leaders. Skilled archer.

Virgos: Courier for the library in Pergamum. Intersex person and son of a Jewish couple who was exiled from Rome by Emperor Tiberius. Known to most people as "Eunuch."

Bracteus: Wealthy olive oil merchant and rising political star in Pergamum. Potential suitor for Domitia. Collects medicines and poisons made from plants.

Batos: Soldier in the Roman auxiliary cavalry. Served in North African provinces of Mauretania and Numidia. Travels with Good News theater company as their watchman.

Claudia: Political leader in Pergamum and mother of Domitia. Organizes imperial festivals and rituals.

Good News Theater Company: Theater troupe that writes and performs plays about Jesus of Nazareth. Learned about Jesus in Thessalonica, where they met Paul. Now travelling down the western coast of Asia Minor.

**Julia Severa: Wealthy benefactor in the city of Acmonia in Asia Minor. Imperial cult high priestess and benefactor of Jewish synagogue. Friend of Domitia and her family.

Pteleah, also known as **Leah:** Head of a creative house in Adramyttium. Develops and produces plays for the elites and for the followers of Jesus.

Ifran: Horse groom at a stable in Assos. Served in the auxiliary cavalry with Batos.

**Emperor Claudius: Roman emperor on the throne during the time of this story (41–54 CE). Scholar and friend of freedmen.

**Emperor Gaius Germanicus: Known by his nickname of Caligula ("Little Boots"). Son of a Roman general and emperor from 37–41 CE.

**Tacfarinas: Trained as a Roman soldier in North Africa. Led an armed rebellion against the Romans. Killed by the Romans in Auzea in 24 CE.

**Incitatus: Favorite horse of Emperor Caligula. Led staged attack over the bay at Puteoli.

**indicates that the individual can be found in historical sources

Prologue

SHE WILLED HERSELF INTO the whirlwind and emerged upright. Now, with the vortex of dust behind her, she paused at the crest of the ridge and surveyed the path below. She followed the path with her eyes, down through a shallow canyon, until it reached a stream and a grove of trees. In the heat shimmer she saw a small house and the vague shape of a tree stump.

A blast of furnace air lifted the long copper hair off her neck. She smelled chestnuts and fire. The sweat on the edge of her ear dripped into the dust. Tongue cracked and dry, she lowered her head. The creak of her knees told her that she was still moving.

The shape ahead had the form of a tree stump, but it straightened its spine and became a man. Thirst forms shapes where there are none. The man was sitting on the ground in the dappled shade of an oak branch. A bucket was on his right, and a fire was in front of him with chestnuts in it. He was peeling the husk off of a chestnut with a knife. He popped one into his mouth and glanced back at her. She thought he smiled, but she could not be sure.

The water called her forward. She stepped up behind him and hovered over the bucket. She had forgotten the smell of water and the coolness of the air around it. Three deep swallows. She raised her head and felt the water drip off her chin. He offered her a peeled chestnut on a flat scarred palm. It tasted rich and smoky.

She studied him. His skin glowed like the winter oak leaves that cling to the branch after others have fallen. Rough tunic the color of bark. Breeches of a horseman. He had a keen type of vigilance, even at rest. He reminded her of a sand cat.

Out of the small house came a man who looked like a woodpecker. His red hair stood on end. Two children followed him and wrestled each other into the stream. They played with the skin of the wolf and pretended to be predators. "She finally came down from the hills," the man said. He approached her and looped a rope around her neck. "We will eat well tonight! I'll go tell the wife. She can make a stew. In a few hours we will eat like kings!"

He turned and entered the house. The man sitting next to her said nothing and waited until the other man disappeared. He loosened the rope and lifted it up over her horns. He tossed it away from them so that it was out of reach. She turned her face toward him. She told him, "Thank you. I will remember you." She took another long drink, turned toward the path that led out of the canyon, and started walking.

The goat remembered the way home. Walk through the day and night. When the sun goes down, look for the star that flickers. Turn where the water turns. Find the mountain ridge that curves toward the sea. Striped hyenas and jackals will follow but keep moving. On the wind will be juniper and apricot. When the cedars rise, she will be close. But she will have to walk through the valley first.

Chapter 1

Domitia

SHE OFTEN FOUND DEATH interesting, but not today. Her husband's funeral could not have been more boring. The imperial rites were complete, and now they were making speeches.

Pergamum knew how to organize a good funeral, especially among the wealthy. As the daughter of an Asiarch, she had negotiated and sometimes physically pushed her way through throngs of admirers and sycophants. They were hungry for power and influence, and they believed her father could give that to them. Unfortunately, for them, her father was still in Rome and unable to return in time. The decision to go ahead with the funeral was not her own, and she didn't care. One day was as good as another.

Standing next to her mother in the front row, as the speeches droned on, she fought the veil that kept blowing over her face. Her mother did the same. Across the crowd, her friend Virgos shot looks at her as the speakers made pretentious claims. He was a head taller than the crowd, and she could easily see his reaction to their grandiose attempts at flattery. He was her lifelong companion, a friend since childhood, and she could tell that he was not bored. He was having fun. It gave him an opportunity to add unspoken commentary of satire and sarcasm. She wished she could have stood by him instead of the front row, where the crowd watched her as much as they did the speaker at the podium.

The speaker was eager for the attention. Thrilled at the political possibilities, Bracteus was relatively new to Pergamum, but he had climbed the rungs of influence with astonishing speed. He had acquired one of the largest olive oil businesses in all of Asia Minor and was recently appointed gynmnasiarch. With money and a new office behind him, he relished this moment for what it could add to his collection. If this were the typical funeral speech, her son would have given the address. She had no son. She had no daughter. The marriage had produced no children, and neither had she. The decision to give this speech to Bracteus was also not her own. She wondered why she was there at all.

He had dressed for the role of a lifetime. He wore an elaborate cuirass, although she was not certain that he had ever served in the military. Without a doubt, he was beautiful physically: striking black hair carefully coiffed, deep resonating voice and cadence that reflected his training in oratory, smooth, well-oiled skin. He was a winner by elite standards, but the script in front of him told her that he could not speak extemporaneously. He kept the script partially hidden, as if it were a scroll accidentally placed near the podium by another. But his mask of effortless composure was wearing thin.

He had stepped up to the podium and opened his arms as if the crowd had erupted in applause. He began: "I approach this task with all humility and gratitude that this privilege was entrusted to me. Of course, my mere words could not improve upon the great deeds of P. Fabius Vesiculus. Nor could my voice loom larger than those who have spoken already today of the man who lies before us. My achievements in the games and now as engineer of the largest and most successful olive oil business compare in only small ways to his favors and benefactions shown to his extraordinary family and this magnificent city.

"It is only fitting that we laud such a fine man and name his numerous public works. His improvements and repairs of the theater stage, for which he earned first seating, brought him the acclaim of our performing artisans. Without his generosity, mimes would have gone hungry and choirs would have lost their voices. Our collective sound, harsh and dissonant now with grief, will rise again to be a light for all of Asia. Regrettably, his early ties to the emperor Gaius were unfortunate, but I will not mention that here. Even when he could only survey the achievements of others, his financial zeal continued. He demonstrated great largesse toward other public works, such as renovations of the baths and free banquets for the disenfranchised. His eye for the lowly would not be deterred, even when his investments could have had more impact elsewhere.

"As colleagues, P. Fabius Vesiculus and I had the best interest of the city as our aim, as we built relationships with prominent leaders around Asia and initiated collaborative efforts with senators from Rome. I carried our joint purpose to Rome and met with our great emperor Claudius. The emperor and I have built a friendship that has created a conduit of goodwill which will continue for decades. If his family would appoint me to continue his negotiations, I would take his name and the city of Pergamum even further to a level of distinction never before seen. When I rejoin my friends in Rome, it will be due only to the wings of the eagle whose life has now ended, who despite his Greek birth, excelled to the ranks of Roman virtue."

A paltry applause arose from the crowd. He paid them to do that, she thought. Can someone please stop him?

Bracteus continued his performance. "I praise today his family: his widow Domitia, so tragically barren and now bravely facing the world without children around her. This tragedy notwithstanding, the utmost wisdom of P. Fabius Vesiculus was demonstrated by his choice of wife, a beauty descended from the heavens, treasure that brings us to our knees, a prize for any victor anywhere. Her delicate constitution, moderation, and restraint are models for all women. I praise too her mother, the exceptional Claudia, who has ushered Domitia through these trials and will no doubt guide her to a successful second marriage. As many of you know, as a child in Aphrodisias, I did not have a mother. She perished during the most sacred duty of childbirth, leaving me to long for the benefits of such a marvelous matron. May their household flourish under her tutelage.

Domitia heard her mother cough softly and felt her hand squeeze her elbow. "Athena, please rescue me," Claudia said into her veil.

Bracteus raised his arms in conclusion. "Inspired by the zeal of P. Fabius Vesiculus, and as those shaped by his example, I offer free olive oil to all participants of the upcoming games to be held in honor of the birthday of Augustus. I will sponsor free banquets for the entire city at the festival both this year and next. I will erect a monument to our magnificent emperor Claudius, the Savior and Benefactor of all humanity and my personal friend, to be placed in the imperial sanctuary. With my army of friends, we join our voices in unison for our most excellent emperor, whose achievements place in shadow even the deceased whom we honor at this assembly."

Domitia asked her mother, "Is he done?"

Bracteus pointed at Virgos in the crowd and said, "You. Eunuch. Bring the tray of oil to me." Virgos turned slightly into the group and pointed at himself, as if to question the recipient of the order. "Yes, you. Eunuch. Bring the tray of my oil to me at the podium now."

Virgos parted the crowd and walked to the tray of faceted glass bottles that had been placed at the edge of the stage. He reached the stage and carefully lifted the tray, but his hands shook and the tray nearly slipped out of his hands The glass bottles clanked against one another. Domitia knew him to have excellent balance and concentration. "What is he doing?" she whispered to her mother.

Virgos took two steps and tripped over the corner of a flagstone. He flopped dramatically and launched the tray of glass into the air. The bottles landed on the stone and splintered in pools of oil. Virgos stood and apologized profusely. "I am so sorry, sir. I am clumsy. Please forgive me. I will return to my place in shame."

Bracteus spat, "You are useless." He faced the crowd and said, "One is forced by incompetence to conclude. May all the sentiments and commitments expressed here today come to pass. Long live Pergamum and long live the Empire. May it bless us all."

"I think he's done," Domitia said. The crowd dispersed with murmurs and small group whispers. She tore the veil off her head. "Publius is dead. The show is over. He has no authority over me anymore."

She did not walk home with the rest of the grieving group. She had to find Virgos and thank him.

Chapter 2

Virgos

"THIS GLUE WILL HOLD," the butcher had said. It was made of boiled sheep hooves. "If you place it directly on the break in the wood and off to either side, it will seal." The butcher seemed proud of his instruction, as if it were original or insightful. Virgos had taken the clay jar with a nod.

Under the table now, in his makeshift office, he was not skeptical of the glue's powerful hold. It made a sucking sound as he pulled it from the open jar with a horsehair brush. The leg would attach to the flat underside of the table as it would attach to the vertical face of a mountain. The table would likely limp because of the break at the joint, but the prophet Jacob had performed mighty works with a limp.

Most of the items in his work area had some sort of wound or wobble. What he called his office, others called a lean-to, or more practically, without recognition of the space as an entity in itself, the back entrance to the storage room of the library. In the beginning, most were surprised to discover that he had made a home there. Now they called out to him as they arrived at the door and found him hunched over scrolls day and night. He repaired what he could. A potter had given him experimental lamps that gave light but would not sell. He found them beautiful. Domitia had given him an unused chair that was more like a throne. He had hauled away trash, rebuilt the slanted roof, stabilized a wall with a new wooden pillar, and even made a window. A dove sat there.

His office had also given the library scribes a place to find him when they needed assistance with variants, marginal notes, and the errors of previous scribes. They needed his assistance often. As a courier and parchment delivery man, he was an unusual choice of consult, but expert nonetheless. It was surprising how few instincts copyists had. He did not resent supplying them. One forms community where it can be found. The noise of the street was comforting to him also. It matched the multiple threads of conversation in his mind.

As he held the leg joint under the table, his hair fell in his eyes. Though fading now, the summer heat made the hair stick to his face. In a brief instant of jest, he regretted taking that Nazirite vow. He would have to borrow some type of hair restraint device from Domitia.

He heard a knock at the wall. He was not ready to let go of the joint, so he responded from underneath the table. "Who is it?"

"It's the Messiah."

Virgos recognized the voice of his friend Zakarias from Alexandria. "In that case, come in," he said, as he poked his head out from underneath the table. He stood and they embraced. Another year had passed, and he looked the same.

Zakarias' eyebrows met at the middle. "Your hair . . . "

"I took a Nazarite vow. I will cut it when I enter the temple in Jerusalem."

"With all that hair, you might not be able to see it," Zakarias quipped.

"I will see it and I will enter," Virgos said firmly. He noticed the bag of scrolls, letters, and speeches that Zakarias had come to Pergamum to deliver. Most would be performed at the festival of Augustus' birthday, he thought, and he would probably be forced to attend.

Virgos leaned against the table gingerly. "Tensions still high in Alexandria?"

"Claudius' edict was vague. He wants to give the impression of tolerance but he's suspicious. I don't mind courier work for that reason. I get to travel, read . . . I even get to steal texts from the library in Alexandria and deliver them to people who will keep them safe." He reached into his leather bag and brought out a new papyrus scroll. He offered it to Virgos, who seized it with enthusiasm.

Virgos held hope at a distance. "Was it sent by . . . "

Zakarias smiled. "It was sent by someone who stipulated that it be brought to you alone and who asked to remain anonymous. Well, scratch that. 'Asked' is not the correct verb. 'Insisted' is more appropriate, with a subtext of 'if you mention my name I will make your life Sheol.'"

Virgos laughed and kept his eyes on the scroll. "I miss her."

"If you ever change your mind, and decide to go to Egypt instead of Israel, you are welcome in Alexandria."

The scroll was newly made of papyrus strips that made a crisp rattling sound. "Wisdom" was written in Greek at the top. The script was legible and clear. A determined sort of lettering. It was her hand, he was sure of it. Slight slant to the left. Minimal marginal notes and errors. She had made up her mind what she would write before she wrote it. What few notes there were, were a result of a mind that did not cease.

"I'll leave the two of you alone."

Virgos looked up and realized that Zakarias had spoken those words. "Thank you, my friend."

Zakarias stepped out into the street. "Until next time."

Virgos sat in his throne and lovingly opened the papyrus treasure. He held it close to the lamp to study it. He thanked the psalmist who gave him words. Let all who breathe praise the Lord. Your word is a light.

Chapter 3

Claudia

SHE HAD A HABIT of talking to letters.

Erecting a funerary monument for a well-respected community leader would have been simple. A few conversations, favors. Convincing all the city's associations to endorse and sign it was another. The death of Domitia's husband happened to coincide with preparations for the birthday of Augustus. The timing gave them an opportunity to link the two into a grand occasion and promote generosity at all levels. But the Jewish association was dragging its feet with regard to the wording on the monument itself. This script would have been ready for the engravers a week ago, were it not for the reluctance of the Jewish leaders to have their name included on it.

Alone in her husband's office—hers more than his—she spoke to the letter. "That is not my problem. I don't need to know details. Yes, the language is firm. 'Well-being of the emperor and his family. The Divine Caesar and the eternal goddess Roma. Sebastos. Son of the Most High God.' Yes, all of that." She paused as her eyes moved down the letter. "Your absence will be conspicuous. Other associations will see that you did not participate. How do you expect to maintain good relationships? This is a privilege. Claim your place in the city." She sighed and looked up at nothing in particular. The Dionysiasts had sent their approval yesterday. Only the Jewish association remained. She may have to move forward without their endorsement.

She tossed the letter on the massive table in front of her. It was piled high with wax seals, ink, parchment, papyri, and small gifts from clients who wanted to be remembered. Management of all matters home fell to her. "Home" was broadly defined, and in this case, more readily extended to the city as a whole. With her husband still away, Bracteus had tried to claim that the funerary monument was his. Soon the public would know it had very little to do with him. That issue would resolve itself. But the delay and argument surrounding the language of the dedication may have to be resolved in ways that were less than ideal. He had also approached her on two occasions and asked about the possibility of marrying Domitia. She shut it down, but he was not deterred.

She looked up to see Domitia, still in her morning gown and carrying a handful of dried apples. She sat in the formal chair in a decidedly informal way: the bottom of one foot on the seat, knee up to her chin, tearing small pieces off of one apple at a time and chewing with her front teeth. She smiled as if she had heard her mother's one-sided conversations. "Can we add what my husband didn't do?"

"Even we cannot afford an inscription that long," Claudia responded. "I have a meeting scheduled with his estate manager this afternoon."

"Thank you," said Domitia. She laid her head back on the chair.

"I commissioned a new hymn for the festival in his honor. I am having a new cameo made. You can wear it at the dedication of the monument." Domitia took another bite of apple as if she had said nothing. "There will be suitors. Bracteus has already spoken to me about the possibility. Since his wife died, he has been eager to remarry. When your father returns, they may make plans."

"A miserable thought. To him, even eulogy is aretology. Did you see his manuscript hidden under the podium? He cannot speak without it. Did he think he was fooling us?"

"I will dissuade him," Claudia announced. I will need leverage to direct him elsewhere, but I will find it."

Into the room swept a confident, well-dressed slave with a letter in her hand. "Ah, my trusted secretary," Claudia said. "Another letter?"

As she swept out, Domitia said with eyebrows raised, "You mean 'slave.'"

"Yes, slave," Claudia said matter of factly. "We have slaves. Every great house does. Do you want to do what they do?" Domitia remained silent as Claudia opened the letter. "It's from Julia Severa."

"What's the news from Acmonia?"

Claudia read aloud: "Julia Severa, servant of Acmonia and appointed guardian of the city. Greetings and condolences to our beloved Domitia in your time of mourning and the uncertainty that follows such a time. The news of your husband's passing distressed us and brought concern for your welfare. Without question your family will guide you through these difficult days and usher you into a new era of joy. As for me and my family, we negotiate the old and the new. We attempt to make peace within the tradesmen's associations and restrain them from injuring one another in word or deed. This has always been our role, and we delight in it.

Developments in Thessalonica have surprised us, however. A few of our leading citizens have returned from Thessalonica and brought with them words of the Jewish teacher Paul of Tarsus. He speaks of the Messiah among us, in these days, in the person of Jesus of Nazareth. Debate about this Paul and this Jesus of Nazareth has reinvigorated discussion and appreciation of Jewish scriptures. This is surely a benefit. I seek to preserve their right to practice their tradition fully. As a tradition of venerable antiquity, it should be respected.

Our concerns center not around the flurry of titles, where to apply them, or the texts that spur such discussion. The titles of Messiah, Christos, Chrestus, even the Son of God, may all be rumblings of the same storm. About that we do not worry. Some of our fellow civic leaders are far too territorial in that regard. Of course I am curious. Is this ancient Judaism, or a novel thing, or yet another ill-advised revolt? But until proven otherwise, we welcome good news from all quarters. It is not in their best interest to be so defensive. As the recent decades have shown us, and future decades will continue to prove, we can thrive together.

However—and this is where we wonder to the point of wakefulness—we have heard that this Jesus of Nazareth is also a crucified criminal. I am incredulous that such a key role would be played by someone who died such a shameful death. Would not those who follow him endure the same fate and the same public opinion? Although we are far from certain if this Jesus was indeed the Messiah, some of my Jewish friends, as well as a few others, persuasively attest on his behalf and earnestly hope that we are now in the days of his reign. Their hope must be nimble, however, in light of his crucifixion. Here I will tell you a secret, dear Domitia. Personally and privately, I would cherish the possibility that the crucified is indeed the Christ, for who else would bring the oblivious to account? Who else could silence those who insist on glory for glory's own sake? I have argued elsewhere that such resources are to be shared and given freely for the benefit of all. Time will tell us who this Jesus of Nazareth is, and we await more news daily.

I close now with thoughts of friendship and hope that we may soon meet. Tatia and Praxias send their love. Julia Severa."

Claudia rested the letter on the table. The news of Jesus of Nazareth seemed far off, like a person shouting in a wind storm. Without comment, they both stood and moved toward the next portion of the day. Domitia turned toward the door and pointed at a portrait of Emperor Claudius on the wall. It was in the process of being repainted. The head had been painted over with a solid beige color so that the body had no head at all. She asked, "Do we really need to keep repainting the emperor's head? Why don't we repaint it as Augustus? You won't need to repaint it every time a new emperor takes the throne or gets damned."

"Your father wanted it repainted," Claudia said, annoyed. "He thought Claudius looked effeminate."

"Repaint it as Augustus Caesar," Domitia said as she left the room. "Isn't he divine? And he's already dead." She stepped around the fountain in the center of the atrium toward her room to change. "I'm going to see Virgos."

Claudia spoke toward Domitia's back as she moved away. "Take a slave with you when you go."

"No," said Domitia, as she walked out and closed the door behind her.

Chapter 4

Domitia

"I COULD BRING YOU another lamp. How do you read in here?" Domitia asked, standing near Virgos in the dim light.

"Who needs a lamp when you have this?!" He was sitting in the ornate chair she had brought him and bent in half over the table. "A new text. Sent to me from Alexandria. It's astonishing. Listen: " . . . blessed is the eunuch who worked or committed no transgression by his hand or considered evil things toward the Lord, for he will be given a select favor because of his steadfastness, and a share to delight in, in the temple of the Lord.'"

Domitia smiled and took a step toward him as he continued to read. "A share in the temple of the Lord, for me! I knew Isaiah wasn't the only one with this vision. Isaiah, you are not alone! Another voice joins your company. Eunuchs with a monument and a name, within the walls of the Lord's house."

Domitia smiled. "Quite a departure from Leviticus."

Virgos stepped away from the desk and paced in a small circle. "The tradition is bigger than my parents said it was. I wish they were alive to see this. They were so certain that people like me should stand aside. When they were kicked out of Rome, they buried their Judaism, and they would not let it breathe. They would not discuss anything," he sighed and sat down again. He spoke deliberately and pronounced each word separately. "The covenant includes me."

Domitia asked, "Am I in it?"

Virgos went back to the papyrus. "Blessed is the barren woman who is undefiled, who has not intercoursed, or had intercourse, in transgression, for she will have fruit at the examination of souls." He smiled proudly. Domitia thought of the ways in which these words did not apply to her, but she did not say anything. His joy was too precious to disrupt.

Virgos was lost in discovery. "Eunuchs, barren women and foreigners are all named and valued here. My parents would not discuss their family names either, but I've been researching my family names. I discovered that I am a Gaul on my mother's side. There is room for all of us! There is room."

From the street, a woman dressed in multicolored sashes motioned toward both of them to come outside. "A play! Come to a play!" Domitia stepped into the doorway and saw a crowd moving together down the street. Virgos rolled the papyrus into a leather carrier and they joined the eager throng. They followed the crowd through the city to the Citadel Gate. A crowd milled around in front of a makeshift wooden stage built in the open space near the Sebastoi.

The event fascinated Domitia. She recognized her seamstress in the group, but most of them seemed to be travelers, a mobile theater company, working the circuit of cities and making money as they go. Resting on the flat wooden stage were four elevated wooden platforms. An actor stepped up onto each platform in preparation for the opening scene. The actors were barely clothed and smeared in charcoal and olive oil so that their skin looked like marble. They assumed the pose of statues and froze as they waited for the play to begin. One appeared to be Augustus, while two others seemed to be Asclepius and Athena. The fourth platform had a wooden cross on it. It was the type that the Romans use for crucifying criminals and bandits. An actor stood in front of it with his arms outstretched and head fallen forward.

A man with a booming voice stepped onto a platform near the side of the stage. "Welcome to all! To those who are present today and those who are not. Galli from Gaul. Trojans from Troas. All those who have followed us here and those who would not know us anywhere. We present to you a play! A pantomime! We tell the story of Jesus the Christ, who took upon himself the sins of all on the cross. Jesus the Christ who ushers in an era of peace and everlasting life. Jesus the Christ as made known to us by the teacher Paul of Tarsus. We will be available after the show to share more about this news of salvation. We can answer any questions you may have. But it is time to start the show. All the way from Thessalonica, the Good News Company presents: Asylum."

The man stepped off the platform and watched with anticipation. From within the audience, an actor shouted and started pushing the crowd forward to make a path. Dressed only in a loincloth, a young man, lithe and lean, spun and ducked through the crowd. He was frightened and hiding behind crowd members as if they would keep him safe. He emerged from the front of the audience as his pursuers appeared. Dressed as Roman soldiers, they were heavily armed and chasing him angrily, as if he had escaped from them. Their weapons clanked against one another as they shoved people to the side.

Another voice from offstage shouted, "The Son of God approaches!" A group of actors in parallel lines marched through the empty space in front of the stage. A chaotic parade ensued, set to a grand series of chord progressions from the horn and flute. The actors were dressed as an emperor and queen, slaves and attendants. They threw homemade coins and flower petals and chunks of bread into the audience. Musicians accompanied the royal entourage but could not drown out the rowdy crowd, who heckled the king and shouted, "Where is the dole? Feed your people with that ring!"

The dancer and his pursuers stopped as the parade progressed and moved out of sight. Crouching behind the last parade musician, the dancer stepped quickly to the statue of Augustus. Domitia leaned toward Virgos and whispered, "That's what they meant by asylum: pleading for freedom from a statue of the emperor." Virgos nodded but could not look away. Following closely, the soldiers tried to capture their prey. The dancer pushed and pulled, leaned and then leaned back, in a struggle against the soldiers. The muscles of his chest rippled over his ribs with strength and poise. It was as if they were connected by an invisible string that released when the dancer broke away. He knelt and prayed and begged toward the statue of Augustus with his hands pressed together, but the statue did not move.

He stepped behind the statue of Asclepius, and the soldiers continued to chase him. He ran around the base of the statue and stumbled, begging to be acknowledged by Asclepius, but the statue remained still. He freed his arm from the soldiers' grip as he knelt again, this time in front of the statue of Athena. She did not notice him. He spun away and knelt in front of the statue of Jesus of Nazareth on the cross. The actor on the cross lifted his head and pulled his arms in off the crossbeam. He extended them to the dancer below as an invitation to stand.

Now down off the cross, Jesus stepped in front of the dancer and shielded him from the soldiers with his body. The soldiers stopped, and the crowd fell silent.

"Disband!" shouted a town guard from the edge of the crowd. The crowd turned toward his sudden exclamation. He was not an actor, but an official guard appointed by the town magistrate to prevent riots and large gatherings. He moved in with a small group of guards and stood on the stage. "Where is your permit?" he shouted toward the actors. "Break it up! Go home!"

The man who gave the spoken introduction to the play stepped onstage. He had an air of authority, as if he were a director. The guard insisted. "Where is your permit? Did the magistrate give you permission to perform here today?"

"Of course," the man said. "It was a verbal agreement yesterday."

The guard laughed. "Yesterday? The magistrate has been in Sardis for weeks. There is no such agreement."

The director started to back away and raised his shoulders in a shrug. "I have good hearing . . . ?" He turned and sprinted away from the stage. Immediately the guards lunged after him. The actors scattered. The musicians grabbed their instruments and ran. The statues jumped off their platforms and ran in all directions. The crowd split into pieces.

Domitia didn't see the company's watchman until he stood on the director's platform and raised his arm straight into the air. He wore a rough, homemade tunic and breeches like someone who had been in the cavalry. The side of his face looked as if it had been burned, and one of ears formed a knob. He whistled one high and piercing note to get the company's attention. He straightened the first three fingers of his hand, with the other two fingers folded under. He twisted his wrist to point in the direction of the open street. He hopped down off the platform and herded the actors and musicians out of the melee. He separated small groups of arguing actors, saying, "Let's go. Keep moving." The two actors who played Augustus and Athena approached Domitia and Virgos, and she was thrilled to be so close to the action. Athena yelled toward the guards, "Theater is not a crime!"

Augustus shouted, "You are the tragedy!" With a slight smirk, the watchman guided them away and disappeared down the street.

As the crowd dispersed, the stage stood empty. Virgos was smiling with an irrepressible joy. "This is the day that the Lord has made," he said, his eyes gleaming.

Domitia squeezed his elbow. "What was that?" she said with a soft laugh.

"Whatever it was, I want to see it again."

"So do I," Domitia agreed. She appreciated the athleticism of dance but had very little experience with it herself. With acting and choreography, the company had created a world without empty babble. They had expressed the ineffable and sublime with a lean and fold of body. They had taken the risk to perform, and they were not ashamed. Would she ever be part of such a movement? Could she ever move like that? The thoughts gripped her and she tucked them away for future consideration.

In the dust, in front of the stage, was a crown. It had been worn by the king in the play's parade. The crown was woven of twigs and a strip of indigo fabric. Domitia picked it up and held it in her hands. She asked Virgos from a distance, "Should we return this?"

Virgos said without hesitation, "Yes. We should return it to them. I will go with you."

Chapter 5

Virgos

Walking through Pergamum was never simply walking. It was ascending or descending. He felt as if he had grown up on a slant. He wondered about flat places and if he would be able to keep his balance on the day when the valleys were exalted and the rough places made plain.

Nearing the entrance of Bracteus' palatial estate, he prepared for the inevitable arrogance. He was sent to pick up a manuscript of the funeral speech in order for it to be placed in the library's collection. Bracteus had wanted it there "for the sake of posterity," and the scribes agreed. His donations would keep them in oil and light for years to come. Their choice made sense on practical and political levels, if not on literary criteria, and Virgos was not asked to provide his opinion on the matter. He was simply a courier.

Leading up to the main entrance was a series of sculptures that recalled the images on the Great Altar in Pergamum. Glorious gods and hybrid monsters were locked in combat. Their swords were raised in what looked to be the final blows of victory for the gods. On the doorstep, a dying Gaul was placed opposite a bound Amazon. Virgos had to stand between them as he knocked on the front door. As he waited, he thought about the air around the estate. It was never free or fresh. Bracteus drugged himself with an old story of dominance, and he seemed to need it.

The heavy door swung open and Virgos saw a familiar face smiling warmly. His friend Arminius said, "Come in! Welcome. I was expecting you." They stepped through the foyer and around the atrium fountain. "How is your foot?" Arminius asked with a mischievous smile. "After your tumble at the funeral, I hope you were not injured. We have seen you step over that flagstone a hundred times."

Virgos smiled. Arminius laughed out loud. "Someone had to stop him," Virgos said. "That speech would have dragged on for days."

"All of us thank you. We owe you a favor." He gestured toward the office door. "He's in there."

Virgos asked, "How is his mood today?"

"He has been working diligently on the written manuscripts of his speech. But otherwise good. Atomia visited earlier today. He is still glowing."

"Atomia was here? The playwright?" Arminius nodded. "Hmm," Virgos pondered aloud and knocked on the door frame.

"Enter now," Bracteus said from behind his desk. His desk was shaped around him like a fort. Storage nooks were built on either side of a large chair upholstered in red brocade. Behind him, on the wall, were three shelves that ran the length of the room. They held a blinding display of gleaming glass bottles. Faceted and smooth, small and large, the bottles were gathered into subgroups and labeled with tags that he could not read at a distance. Other bottles and jars were made of clay, alabaster, and stone, all grouped separately and labeled.

"I told the scribes to send a man for my manuscripts, not a eunuch," Bracteus said.

"I am a man."

Bracteus shook his head in exasperation. "Here is my speech. I made two copies. Tell them to place it in front so that it can be seen."

"I will," Virgos said flatly. He gestured toward a small pink alabaster bottle at the corner of the desk. "Is this a new addition to your collection?"

"It was a gift from Atomia." Bracteus blushed as he spoke.

"I heard her theater troupe was producing magic shows now," Virgos said.

"They have resorted to popular magic, unfortunately. But she came to me today about funding for a new work. A drama featuring me as epic hero and central character. It will showcase my prowess in all its forms. I have agreed to sponsor it. It will be performed all over Asia."

"Congratulations," Virgos said.

Bracteus nodded as if he had merited the sentiment. "She assured me that no man will be my equal."

"Without a doubt," Virgos responded. He gestured toward the shelves of bottles. "Tell me about your collection," he asked.

Bracteus gestured toward the shelves. "This is my hellebore. I have spent years amassing samples of each type from all over the world. Powders and liquids. Harvested at different times and in different ways. Atomia tells me that her gift is a particular rarity from Mount Ida."

"What purpose does your collection serve?"

"Hellebore is a mystery to physicians," Bracteus explained. "It has many surprising applications, but the results are not controlled. It can be used as medicine or poison. It can cause stupor or paralysis, or it can clear the mind. Depending on the type, amount, or when or how it was collected and processed, it can kill an elephant or cure madness."

"Which goal is yours?" Virgos asked.

"I have killed elephants. A human male did not survive one dose. But I have yet to cure madness. Hysteria, hallucinations . . . these have eluded me. Hellebore could be an effective treatment, but I have not been able to prove it."

"An admirable pursuit," Virgos said.

Bracteus nodded without acknowledgement that the comment might have barbs attached. "It is," he said. He placed the manuscripts at the edge of the desk. He stood, turned his back to Virgos, and tidied the bottles on the shelves.

Virgos stood in the silence for a brief instant. "I will take these to the library," he said toward Bracteus' back. "Placement of them within the library, however, is not up to me."

Bracteus dismissed him with the back of his hand. As Virgos turned toward the exit, he deftly lifted the pink alabaster bottle off the desk. As he walked out, he felt it resting in the corner of his pocket.

Chapter 6

Domitia

DOMITIA HEARD VIRGOS BEHIND her in the street, but the words were not distinct. Crown in hand, she slowed and waited for him to catch up. "Walking with you is like chasing the wind," Virgos said.

She laughed and apologized. "I just want to find them," she said. The two of them were walking in the direction of the play they had seen, hoping to catch a glimpse of the theater company. It was possible that they had already left town, but she wanted to find out more. The director, if that's who he was, said in the introduction to the play that they would answer questions. Virgos pulled his hair out of his eyes and wiped sweat off his temple. "You're getting shaggy," she said in the easy manner of old friends.

"You may call me Samson," he responded.

A priest and a bull on the way to sacrifice separated Domitia and Virgos in the street. They stood on either side as the imposing figures passed, and then resumed their walk in the center of the street. "Do you think they will still be here? Have you ever heard Paul of Tarsus, or Jesus of Nazareth?"

"I have not heard of either one, but the themes of the play were familiar."

"Have they written anything? Have you seen anything in the library from them, or heard of any correspondence from them?"

"Nothing. But the library is large, and some do not find my presence helpful."

Domitia saw the dancer first, fully clothed now, leaning forward into a heated argument between a woman next to him and a shop owner inside a storefront booth. Next to the dancer was the watchman who herded the troupe to safety after the play. She remembered his whistle and the mended burn on his face. Walking toward them now, she noticed bright silver threads in his close-cropped black hair. She knew the booth and the owner well. He sold purple fabric to the wealthy of the city, and thought more of himself because of it. This might be the source of tension.

As the distance between them narrowed, she inhaled deeply and pulled her shoulder blades together. She softened and shortened her footsteps and coordinated them into a confident heel-toe rhythm. She lengthened her neck and outstretched her arm. "How can I be of assistance?"

The owner said emphatically, "I will not sell to these vulgar people."

"What are they attempting to buy?" she asked.

"Two remnants of my best purple fabric. The dye came all the way from Mauretania. It is my right to refuse." He gripped the fabric tightly against the table top.

"I am here with a request from my mother. I would like to buy two remnants of your best purple fabric," Domitia stated calmly. She held herself still and kept her shoulders back. You will relent, she thought. I will win this one.

"Do you expect me to believe that is a coincidence? Are you associating with actors now?"

"I will associate with whom I please. Perhaps my family can as well. We can take our money elsewhere," Domitia did not waver in her gaze. The owner released his grip on the fabric and offered it to her. She laid coins on the table equaling more than twice the amount of the fabric's value. She gestured toward the street and spoke to the group. "Shall we walk?"

"I apologize for such ill treatment. I am happy to support your creative work," Domitia said to the woman and dancer.

She responded without deference. "Thank you. I can pay you."

"No," Domitia said. "It is a gift. In fact, it is you I have come to find. I wanted to return your crown. I saw your play, and I cannot stop thinking about it."

The woman smiled at her. They were the same height, but the woman was probably twice her age. Domitia felt as if the woman was smiling directly into her face, without pretension or affectation. She said, "Follow me. Our troupe will meet soon. You are welcome to join us."

Led by the watchman, they traveled in a loose group down the hill toward the lower agora. Domitia elbowed Virgos gently. His eyes had an eager look, as if he were ready for trouble. Winding through gates and between storage areas, they moved toward a grain warehouse. The wheat had been emptied, and the next shipment had not yet arrived. She could hear short bursts of song, exclamations, and a duet with horn and cithara that was not going well.

The inside of the warehouse was lit with lamps. The windows were small and set high, with streams of light beaming down onto the floor below. She savored the creative energy inside. She recognized two actors who had played statues, wiped clean of their makeup of ash and oil and working out the steps to a new dance. Two others were playing with sheaves of wheat and making each sheaf bow to one another. Off to the side were platforms from the play, carpenter's tools, and the beams that had formed the cross. Even the particles of grain dust seemed to play in the air.

The director stepped to the center of the room and motioned toward the two visitors. "Welcome," he said.

Virgos spoke to the group with a confidence that surprised her. "We saw your play. We would like to know more."

The director nodded. "Please stay. Join the riot." He turned toward the group and asked for their attention. "Everyone, can I have your attention please. I want to review our play design and think about whether or not a pantomime is the best choice for us. We all know that it was cut short by the warden. The minimal dialogue meant that the conversation afterwards was more important. We did not have the opportunity to do that. Any comments on this?"

Voices rose from the group, directed toward him and each other.

"People like mime, but it works better for a story that the audience already knows."

"Will they know who Jesus of Nazareth is? The introduction from the emcee does not include everything."

"They can see the cross. That's who Jesus is."

"They did not get it. Did you see the audience? They were not deep thinkers."

"Are they ever?"

Virgos raised his hand and his voice. "Some of them are." A few group members acknowledged his comment with nods as the discussion continued.

"If most of our audience did not get it, we need to change the play. That is why we do what we do. So that the world will know." The director seemed to want to conclude the topic. "It was the first time we performed it. We can talk more about this, but for now let's move on.

"The original score was beautiful. Thank you. The parade accompaniment was particularly effective. My only question is how to increase volume." The musicians disagreed and seemed concerned.

One of them raised her hand. "If we increase volume, we would lose nuance. Also, are there any plans to perform in an odeon?

"I am working on it. Maybe. But is not all space sacred?" The director smiled and raised his arms. "Is not God the maker of all things, sky, stone, and earth?"

The musician groaned. "Yes, but the acoustics are better in an odeon."

"We will adapt. We can perform anywhere, but I will keep your suggestion in mind. We want to thank our dear friend Batos." Applause and acclaim rose as they turned to face the watchman, who stood near the door. "He kept us safe on the journey from Troas to Pergamum. He guided us through the recent disruption and all the others we caused. We were not successful in convincing him to join a play and get on stage, but perhaps someday he will. He should have retired from the military earlier and spent more time with us." He shook his head in mock protest. "He will stay here in Pergamum and rejoin us when we swing back through the area."

Shouts of protest erupted. "Don't leave us, Batos!"

He spoke with one hand raised. "I'll be in the stable."

"We are on our way to Smyrna today," the director said. "I want to talk to the playwrights about our performance there. Everyone else, there will be notes, but they will be great. There will be a tower, a golden calf, and if we can find a wall, we can play with Nehemiah. I'm excited about it. Good things coming our way. That will be all for now. Let's load up. David, do you need help with the cross beams? No? Let's be on our way. Good News Company, what do we say?"

The group responded with a rousing unison. "Not By Word Alone!"

The director repeated it. "Not By Word Alone. Thank you."

The group broke into smaller groups and started carrying props and instruments out to a wagon in the street. Domitia and Virgos were surrounded by the group but did not know what to do. She caught the eye of the director. "We have questions. Is there anyone who can talk to us?"

"We have to get on the road. The best thing for you to do is to find Paul. He was our teacher. He came from Judaism and knows The Story. He might still be in Thessalonica. That is the best place to start." He climbed into the wagon, while others mounted the horses that were waiting next to it. The wagon started moving.

"Wait!" Domitia called after them. "I have your crown!"

The director called back to her. "Keep it. It is a gift."

Chapter 7

Virgos

HE RAN HIS FINGERS across the fine grooves of the papyrus. The edges were crisp and sharp. Someone had cut down the reeds and and laid them in strips to dry with mathematical precision. He whispered a prayer of thanksgiving for this person, rolled the scroll carefully, and placed it into a leather case he had made for special deliveries.

Lifting the strap over his head and across his body, he took a step back from the table. Shaped like a cylinder, the case was made of tooled bull leather with a matching lid that took him months to perfect. The fit was imperative. It must seal out insects, moisture, and other interested parties. There was no question that the Wisdom scroll from Alexandria belonged in it. The text unfurled with each read like a rosebud. Each image built upon the other until he could not contain his delight. Yet this text had incisors. Its critique bit hard and drew blood. Occasionally he had to sit back from the table and summon all his wits to interpret it. The hope it bore lifted him and became his companion. The prophet Isaiah, his treasure and black pearl of astonishing beauty, had done the same.

He thought he might find Domitia at the practice courtyard. One day out of every week, the walled courtyard was reserved for her alone. Having a private space for archery was one of the benefits of her birth. Her father had arranged for it. She had fallen away from archery as a married woman and used the space at uneven intervals. He suspected that her husband had disapproved of it, but she had not said as much. As a widow, she was free to resume, if only in private.

He wanted to show her a passage in the scroll about an arrow and its target. The coincidence of text and current moment pleased him. The reference to an arrow was part of a larger series in the text about the futility of arrogance, and she would appreciate its sharp edge. He would need to enter the courtyard quietly so that if she were preparing for a shot, her concentration would not be disturbed. As he expected, when he entered the courtyard, her arrow was loaded. Her hair was pulled back tightly and knotted behind her head, in the style of the exhibitions she performed during festivals and diplomatic visits. She was focused on the target. Her left arm held the bow straight out in front of her, and she drew back the string with her right hand, so that the string touched the center of her mouth.

He stood quietly, but she stopped the draw and let the bow fall to her thigh. Turning around angrily, she almost spoke. As she recognized him, she let out an exasperated breath. "I thought you were a man," she said.

He looked up at the sky and sucked on the end of his tongue. It was as if he were the target.

An apology flooded out of her. "I am sorry. I thought you were one of those soldiers who hangs around and tells me what to do."

Virgos did not move. He stared at the sky and considered how to respond.

"I am sorry. That was cruel. You did not deserve it."

He lowered his eyes and looked down at her. He allowed his height and his face to speak for him. He saw her regret and her restlessness. "I wanted to show you a passage in the Wisdom scroll."

She motioned toward the half wall where they could sit and examine it together. "Show me," she said. They sat, but he did not take out the scroll. The time was not right. He would wait.

"I am missing every shot today," she said. "I am doing what I always do."

"Where is your mind?" he asked.

"Not on archery. That much is obvious." She paused. "What lies ahead for me here? Tournaments that I am not supposed to win for political purposes? Another strategic marriage? This cannot be all there is."

"I know that this is not all there is. We tell ourselves the world is better when it is named and categorized. There are other voices. Other boats."

"Weeks ago, we had never heard of Paul the teacher or Jesus of Nazareth. Weeks ago, you did not have your rosebud scroll, and look what it means to you now." She turned toward him. "What if we left?"

"Where would we go?"

"Did you see how excited that theater group was? How committed they were to the message of Jesus of Nazareth? Imagine what it would be like to be part of something so life-giving and creative. Remember the introduction to the play, and the play itself? A crucified criminal who could do what the gods could not do. My mother and I received a letter from a friend in Acmonia, and she had heard of Jesus of Nazareth too. And in Thessalonica! The troupe just came from there. The pieces fit together."

Virgos felt his frustration rise. "Do you think this wider world will rescue you from your tricliniums? Is reclining with wealthy politicians not your style? Would you rather barley and mustard and the smell of piss on your hands?"

Domitia agreed more quickly than he thought she might. "I am naïve. I know that. But at least they are following something that is real."

"You do not know what is out there. You have not seen cruelty," Virgos let the words reach the bottom of his voice.

"You don't know what I have seen," she said slowly. "And you are not my father."

"I am not anyone's father."

They sat together in the cleft created by their words. Following fragments of a gospel seemed like venturing out onto a slender branch. She continued, as if she saw an open window. "Why would you want to stay here? You heard the group say that Paul came from Judaism. Learning more about your tradition has been your goal as long as I have known you. Imagine if we could meet Paul. You could have someone to argue with! Someone who could keep up with you. Someone for you to defeat in an argument."

Virgos smiled at the affection in her comment. "That is more likely. But what if Paul's good news is not good news for me?"

She shrugged with one shoulder. "How will you know otherwise?"

"I want to go to Jerusalem, not Thessalonica."

"We can go there, too. Why not? We can go anywhere. We could go to the edge of the world. I have money. Come with me." she said. He noticed that her mind was now present. She was a force that he could only rarely deny.

"Run like sparks through stubble," he said. "Who would show us the way? I have never left Pergamum, and you have been only as far as Ephesus. We have no idea what roads to take."

She was confused by the reference to stubble. "Let's go," she continued. "Let's find someone who can take us to Thessalonica. Didn't the group have a watchman with them? Wasn't he going to stay in Pergamum? What was his name? Batos?"

Virgos let out a long slow breath. "I hope it doesn't take us forty years to get there."

Chapter 8

Domitia

HE WAS NOT IN the stable. They had asked at nearly every booth. They had stopped people in the street to ask if they had seen any members of the theater troupe. The upper agora was crowded with people, but none of them seemed to know anything. "Let's go down the hill," Virgos said. At the corner of the main road of shops, she nearly collided with a runaway pig. An angry man with a rope followed. Virgos pulled her out of their path so that they would not knock her to the ground.

"Thank you. I wasn't looking," she said, still not looking.

He nodded casually. "Caring for widows and orphans. That is what I do."

She shook her head with amusement but did not stop searching. "There," she says, pointing at the leather repair shop ahead. Batos was sitting on the booth table, facing the street. He was barefoot, and his feet did not reach the ground. He was talking animatedly to the leather repairman, who stood behind the table, pounding nails into the bottom of his hobnail boots. Batos was clearly telling a story that made both of them laugh. He turned the top half of his body sideways so he could look at the repairman and talk with his hands.

As they approached, she could hear them speaking in another language. It sounded like Hebrew. She did not know Hebrew, but she had heard Virgos speak it. It made her even more curious. The watchman had a burn from his right cheekbone to his ear. There was a smooth knob where his ear had been, as if the ear had folded over itself. Down his neck to the top of his shoulder and under the neckline of his tunic, the burn was edged in carmine red but had healed long ago. He wore the breeches of a cavalry man. The woolen cloak next to him on the table was soft and showed signs of wear. A custom-made knife lay next to him on the table. Something had been carved into the grip.

Virgos greeted them in Hebrew, and they both replied in kind. She introduced herself in Greek. "My name is Domitia, and this is my friend Virgos. We saw your play. We would like to meet Paul of Tarsus. We heard he was in Thessalonica. We would like to go to Thessalonica and we would like you to take us there." The words came out of her mouth like a drumbeat. He did not seem offended.

He smiled at them both. "I've never met Paul."

"Weren't you in Thessalonica, with the theater troupe?" she asked.

"No. I met them in Troas. But I know the way."

She was conscious of the banging of the hammer and the noise of the street. "Is there somewhere we can talk?"

As he listened, he lowered his chin and looked through the tops of his eyes. "We can talk right here. My boots aren't done yet. I don't know if I can answer your questions, but I can take you to someone who can."

Virgos asked, this time in Greek. "How did you meet the theater troupe?"

Batos responded easily, as if they had known one another for years. "I was in Troas. I had just retired from the auxiliary cavalry. I like being on the move, and I believed in what the troupe was doing. So I agreed to travel with them."

"Were you an officer?" Domitia asked.

"No," he said. "I was never that kind of hungry." Domitia suppressed a smile. He looked at her calmly. "Why do you want to go?" he asked. "Are you running away from something, or toward something?"

"Both are blended together. Is that a problem?"

"Not at all," he said, moving his head slightly back and forth. "And you?" he asked Virgos. "Why do you want to go?"

"I am going to Jerusalem," Virgos said.

He lifted his chin slightly. "Jerusalem is the other direction."

"I may wander, but I will get there," Virgos responded firmly.

Batos nodded. The decision had been made. "We'll stay to the east and off the main road." The leather repairman handed him his boots, and he held them in his lap with one hand. "We'll travel through Adramyttium and Assos. We'll go on horseback. I will meet you outside the Citadel Gate tomorrow at sunrise. Bring only one or two items each." He hopped down off the table and faced them both. "I'll see you then."

Domitia and Virgos glanced at one another and understood that the conversation was over. "We will see you tomorrow," Virgos said, backing away. Domitia knew it would not be difficult for her to decide what to bring. She would bring her bow.

Chapter 9

Claudia

Kronos did not receive enough recognition for his ability to torture. Extending time was a brutal method of subjugation. Claudia was forced to wait through it, as if it would have no end. She paced around the pool at the center of the atrium and recalled the answers she was given earlier in the day. No one had spoken to Domitia. Someone may have seen her near a leather repair booth, but the booth was closed when she had gone to inquire about it. The archery courtyard was empty. Her room was as she had left it. Her bow stood on end in the foyer. It was nearly sunrise.

Claudia was able to use the waiting time to complete tasks in preparation for Augustus' birthday, but all that could be done was done. Pulling people forward was the worst part of her responsibilities. Nearly always, she was waiting for someone else to do something so that she could finish it. Why were others so slow? Why did she have to work with others in general? She noticed the pattern of questions before she spoke them aloud, but there were no answers either way.

The fountain made the same gurgle it had made an hour ago, and it would still make the same sound hours from now. The mosaic floor was still missing an eye for the dolphin. That was something she could do. She could contact the artisan again so that he would bring the dolphin an eye.

She understood that Domitia had been restless. The riot in the street in front of the Sebastoi had excited her, but that group had since disbanded. Her first marriage had disappointed most everyone involved with it, and Bracteus was maneuvering to be her second husband. She needed leverage in order to keep him out of the hunt for her daughter. He had few political weaknesses and maximized the strengths he had: relationships from his upbringing in Aphrodisias, and considerable skills at creating conflicts among adversaries and then slipping out of the middle, only to watch them destroy each other. If all else failed, he had money to persuade the reluctant.

Domitia would never agree to marrying him. She would rather run. Claudia would be quick to support her, but it would tear her heart out to do so. Perhaps there was a diplomatic mission that would benefit from the presence of local royalty. A visit to Julia Severa's house perhaps. Anything to buy time until she could dig up a relic that would haunt him. Bracteus was smart, but he was a boy. If she found what she needed, she could bring about his public demise without being known as the instigator of it. She needed to move quickly. Her husband would be home soon, and he would not approve of her pursuit. Better that he did not know.

The door swung open and Claudia stood immediately. It was Domitia. Her auburn braids were falling out their coils. Virgos, tall and angular, stood near her. He was her constant companion since they were children. They were siblings, both her children, drawn to each other but from such different circumstances. They were out of breath. Domitia did not pause in the foyer. "I have to go," she said, as she trotted toward her room. Virgos stood awkwardly and shifted his weight. Both knew the significance of the moment, but the words would not fit in the time allowed. Domitia returned with a small bag.

"Where is my bow?" she asked. Claudia nodded toward the bow behind her. Domitia picked it up and they faced one another.

The decision to run had already been made. Any attempt to convince her otherwise would have no effect. "Which way will you go?" Claudia asked.

"North," she said simply.

"I will tell everyone that I sent you south, on a diplomatic mission," Claudia was already thinking of the ways she could give that impression to nosy on-lookers.

"He will look for me everywhere," Domitia said.

"I will do what I can to deter him," Claudia reassured her.

The sound from the fountain seemed to grow louder.

"Tell me we will see each other again," Claudia stated, attempting to control her emotions.

"I can't do that, Magna," she said, using the nickname she gave her mother as a child. "But I will try."

Claudia stepped behind her to pick up a quiver of arrows. "I had new arrows made," she said, as she handed them over.

"Thank you."

"I will be here," Claudia said. How she wished time would stretch out now.

"I know," Domitia said as she was moving away. She and Virgos walked out the door, and it closed behind them.

Only a few minutes before, Claudia had sat in that chair, and now she returned to it with a twisted gut. Athena and all gods, gods of every era and country, above and below, please protect my daughter and bring her back. The thought of sitting made her groan. She could not stay here. Night walks proved dangerous for some, but at this point, she did not care.

She pulled a veil over her head and started to walk. She had grown up here in Pergamum, and she was now a respected leader. The streets and alleys were her own. She walked to the upper stoa near the temple of Athena, and heard the sounds change inside the long hallway. Despite its length and the space that it claimed, it felt sheltered. She studied the statues of kings, politicians, gods, and goddesses that lined the back wall. Telemachus stood on her left, followed by every recent emperor except Gaius Caligula, whose status had been removed and undoubtedly used as fill for a new building somewhere in the city. The artisans had varying levels of skill, some forgettable, and others pushing forward into new eras of sculpture. The bust of Bracteus stood on her right. She knew that artisan well, and he had made a truly beautiful thing. His craftsmanship was exquisite. Bracteus' hair was tousled in the style of Attalus I, with lifelike curls and an aristocratic profile. It was made of the finest marble available. If only the subject were different.

She was studying the jawline when she heard, "You who are simple, turn in here!" She stepped instinctively behind a column to listen undetected. The voice was close, but she had not heard anyone nearby.

"Stolen water is sweet! Turn in!"

Claudia leaned around the column. She saw an old woman, real but almost ghostlike, standing with a man. Her gray hair was falling out. What remained was braided into an elaborate knot under a saffron veil. She wore dangling gold earrings, each in the shape of a human head. With her face in the middle, she looked like Hecate, facing all directions all at once. Makeup was smeared around her eyes. Her knotted limbs jutted out from underneath a torn and dirty dress. A small dog sculpture stood at her feet, next to a strigil and a row of small glass and alabaster bottles.

Claudia recognized the man by his profile because it was staring at her in marble as well. It was Bracteus. He was arguing with her in angry hushed tones. "Mother! I told you to be silent!" The voice confirmed that it was him, but he had stated many times that his mother had died. "Just take your medicine! I will be back. But do not say that you know me."

One column at a time, Claudia stepped quietly forward so that she could hear, and leaned around. The argument continued. The woman's voice was shrill and frenzied. "Do not forsake me to the land of the dead! I will cast a spell on all who oppose you! My son! Won't you speak with your mother?"

Bracteus seized her by the elbow. "Do not speak of me to anyone. I will bring more medicine tomorrow." Claudia leaned back so that the column obscured her and hoped he would not walk toward her. His footsteps faded. She breathed a sigh of relief.

She looked at the marble bust of her adversary. Now she had the leverage she needed to bring him down off his pedestal. He had lied to the funeral assembly and to countless others on his rise to fame. His mother was not dead. She was mad. She dressed as Hecate and loitered around the stoa at night. Whatever he had given her as medicine, it had failed to cure her. What would he do to protect his secret? Marry someone other than her daughter? Leave the city entirely? Claudia was eager to find out.

She circled around through a back alley to the theater. She remembered another bust, a twin to this one, that he had placed near the upper entrance of the theater. If he wanted to look down on the city, she would make that happen.

The height of the theater and its steep incline had always made her dizzy. Undaunted, she continued through the narrow arch of the entryway. She stood at the top of the stairs near the bust and the pedestal underneath. Away from Bracteus was the safest place for her daughter. But Claudia had invested in this city. Pergamum was her home.

With a visceral roar, she shoved the pedestal toward the theater stairs. She watched the bust tip and begin to fall. Tumbling end over end, the statue spun in the air and landed on the stone of the aisle. The head separated from the neck with a muted crack. As the smaller pieces shattered, they made pitches of sound that grew higher and higher. She watched them splinter until the marble lay still and all recognizable pieces were broken.

No, he would not wrest this city from her. She would stay and fight.

Chapter 10

Virgos

Virgos studied the full, ripe sack of testicles under the horse's belly. "At least one of us is intact!" he shouted.

Domitia had no interest. "Do you ever stop thinking about that?"

"No," Virgos said. He stepped up on a boulder and threw a leg over the sorrel stallion. Their tempers had been short all morning. He was mulling over the decision to leave and silenced any concerns about it within himself. She might be doing the same. But he could not resist the temptation to continue. "It is an easy thing for you to dismiss. You are the norm."

"I am unable to have children. I am not the norm." She gripped the reins tightly so that she did not shout the words. She settled her bow behind the saddle and refused to look at him.

Batos stepped into the tension and mediated. "The horses know the way. You will not need to use the reins very often, unless they get distracted. Even then, the reins might not make a difference. Trust them. They are sure-footed." Smaller than most horses he had seen, they had long, thick manes and well-trimmed hooves. Each one had a high pommeled saddle and fringed blanket underneath. Virgos noted that Batos' saddle had the most wear but did not have any stirrups.

"Where did you get your horse?" Virgos said. The chestnut mare was a beauty, and her eyes followed the slightest movement.

"She is her own horse," he said, tightening the girth on the gray mare next to Domitia. "But I brought her mother with me from Mauretania when I retired. She was great at long distances. This one is a better climber." He spoke more freely than he had up to this point. "She chooses a good line up and down. She knows which paths will hold and which ones will give."

Virgos watched Batos as he checked hooves and girths one last time. Not one movement was wasted. His skin was like burnished bronze, and the burn on his face had its own sheen. The left side of his body was significantly more muscular than the right. At his waist hung a custom-made knife, holstered in a homemade belt. The combination of muscle and weapon gave him a confident asymmetry.

He leaned over at the waist near the gray mare. He wove his fingers together into a basket and offered Domitia a step into the saddle. She lifted her foot but did not lift it high enough. He had to lower it for her to step into it and raise her other leg over the saddle. "Don't you dare say that I am short," she said, grasping the reins.

"I wasn't going to say anything," he said. He leapt into his own saddle with no need for assistance. All three started moving simultaneously and unbidden.

"Depart out of your land, and out from your kin, out of your father's house, and into the land that I will show you, and I will make from you a great nation," Virgos spoke Genesis as a prayer. His prayer was just as much for God to show him the land as it was for a great nation. This journey to Thessalonica was risky at best. At least it was for him. Domitia seemed more certain.

Behind Batos on the path, Virgos studied the weapons Batos had attached behind his saddle. He had two short javelins, but no bow or sword. Seeing the weapons now, the asymmetry made sense. His left shoulder was heavily muscled from years of throwing. He wore his dagger on his left side as well, which gave him another weapon he could easily throw. His right side was clearly capable, but no match for the power coiled in his left. "Did you say you were in the auxiliary cavalry?" Virgos asked. "Where did you serve?"

"Ammaedara, initially, with the Third Legion." Batos said without turning around. The horse slowed so that they could walk side by side. "Riding the plateaus and the mountains. Then I was in Auzea for a while. I was in Volubilis when Ptolemy was murdered."

Virgos was surprised by the distance. "Those cities are on the frontier. Numidia and Mauretania. Where were you born?"

"Galatia," Batos said simply.

Virgos pursued the mystery. "Did you choose the frontier? Were there not places closer to home?"

"I didn't want to be closer to home. I left when I was in my teens. I drifted around for a while and found work on a grain boat to Numidia. Enlisted in the auxiliary when I got there. Served my twenty five years and came up here. A lot of men stayed and made money in the animal trade. I didn't want to do that."

Domitia had been listening. "Did you get your Roman citizenship after you were discharged?" she asked.

"No," he said, looking back at her. "I never went to the ceremony. Never bought the diploma tablet."

"But the privileges that citizenship entails . . . you could have . . . " Her voice sounded perplexed. Batos didn't answer.

Virgos thought he had not heard her question and had questions of his own. "How did someone from Galatia find his way to Numidia?"

Batos interrupted crisply, "I told you already." He clucked his tongue, and the mare sped up so that they were leading a single file line. The movement ended the conversation. Fascinated, Virgos knew he would find another opportunity to ask. For now, they were strangers in transit, listening to the sounds of hooves on dust.

Chapter 11

Batos

THE HEAT ON HIS eyelids woke him. The sun had peaked and started its descent. He was lying on his back in a dry lake bed. The water had evaporated long ago and left a crust of salt on the clay. His shoulders were pinned down at the blades and partially buried. Twisted at the waist, his legs were bent and lay off to the right, one knee on top of the other. It was as if he had fallen from a great height and the sun had baked him into clay.

From the feel of his mouth, he had been without water for one day. He could raise his head, and his forearms up to the elbows, but the rest of his body would not move. Dried clay has stiffened his hands, and his knife was out of reach.

He raised his head to survey his surroundings. He was alone on a plateau. Off to his left, at about one hundred paces, he saw a statue of a lion. Polished and gleaming, the lion was carved from lapis luzuli. She was lying on her stomach and resting on her elbows. Her chin was raised and her eyes were closed.

Neck straining from the tension, he laid his head back on the clay. He heard a strange metallic sound. A small clink of metal. He raised his head again and felt a gust of wind cool the right side of his face. The lion seemed to turn her head slightly into the wind. She raised her chin, and her rib cage rose and fell. She was no statue. She was alive and breathing, and she was downwind. She was smelling him.

He tried to free himself again from the hard clay but he could not. The lion stood up in one swift movement and turned toward him. He heard the metallic sound again, this time at rhythmic intervals. He fought the hypnotic pull of her shoulders and the jarring, dissonant clank that did not belong. It was not the rhythm of the hunt but a victory she had already won. He was blinded by the sun on the lapis, a brilliant cobalt blue veined with gold, and the shadow of her mighty head moved alongside her. Her feet curved inward slightly as she walked. The metallic sound was a shackle on one foot. It clanked as it spun.

Slowly she walked the length of his body and stood so that her head hung over his face. Her eyes were rimmed in black. Red salt gathered in the corners of her mouth. Her teeth were like knives of yellow jasper, and her eyes were like amber fire. A piece of her ear was missing. She had a diagonal scar across her chest, as if a blow had opened the stone, and the stone had healed itself. The edges held together like a seam. The shackle on her foot had not been broken. It had worn thin to the point of breaking.

"Whom do you seek, Roman?" she asked.

"I am not Roman."

She looked down his body and up to his face again. Something flickered across her face. "Your uniform does not fit," she said. Her voice was like the underbelly of the ocean in his ears. "Take my words back to those little boys playing desert: Roma is dead. I am older than your jewels and more ancient than your dolls. I was here when the mountains were shaped. I was here before water rose up from the ground. I will be here when your meat rots and your memory scatters. Your scepter has no meaning. You will not conquer me."

As she turned away from him, the dust on her paws scattered, and the clank of the shackle resumed. The brilliant blue of her body glowed as she walked into the ripples of heat and disappeared into the south.

He awoke with his chest full of air. He quickly looked around and then at the night campfire. He had been dreaming of the lion again.

He let out the air. His shoulders were not pinned down, and he was resting on a horse blanket. It was a dark night with no stars. Water was nearby. The horses were nearby. He could hear each of them. His two travelling companions were sleeping lightly, end to end, around the embers of the fire.

He stood up, wiped the sweat off his face, and carefully stepped around the piles of human things they had created on the trail: tack, cooking utensils, food, a few belongings. He turned to the north and then to the west instinctively. He did not know why he did it. An involuntary way of orienting himself. He walked through a gap between scrub bushes until he could see the horizon. The sea was out there, but he could see only empty space. A moth fluttered off a twig into the air in front of him, followed by a bat.

He sat on a flat stone and watched the dark. A horizontal streak of lightning stretched across the sky. Its angles formed a crooked ladder. "Lead on," he said softly. His heart had slowed to its normal beat. What was that look in the lion's eye when he told her that he was not Roman? Recognition? Satisfaction? Kinship? She travelled with him. He would have time to consider it.

He heard a horse behind him. A playful type of pawing. She did that sometimes when she wanted something to do. Before he stood up, he checked the bottoms of his boots for clay.

Chapter 12

Virgos

WHAT IS THE WISDOM of trying to read on horseback? For Virgos, the movement soothed him and helped him consider. Freed of the responsibility of reins, he had unrolled the scroll across the pommel and followed the text line by line. His mind could follow its own path.

He chose a particular reference and sat back to let it settle within him. The handwriting was smeared slightly, but it appeared to say "It was she who rescued a righteous man when the ungodly were being destroyed. He escaped the fire that descended upon the five cities." "She" was undoubtedly Wisdom as an entity and a force. "The righteous man" could be Abraham or Daniel. If Abraham, the five cities would be only four: Sodom, Gomorrah, Admah, and Zeboiim. If Daniel, the reference to five cities made less sense, unless the author is recalling kingdoms, or rulers, such as Nebuchadnezzar, Belshazzar, Belshazzar's queen, Darius, and Cyrus. Abraham was probably the man identified here.

"But Daniel escaped the fire," Virgos said aloud, looking down at the papyrus. "He would not worship the golden statue. He walked around in the fiery furnace, and he lived. That much is clear." His mind savored the palimpsest of themes in Wisdom and Daniel: idolatry, resistance, and prophetic speech. Smiling, he looked up to see Batos riding next to him. He saw the burn on Batos' face and bit his lower lip. Batos had not spoken of the burn, and Virgos had not intended to pry open a possibly painful subject. He had not been thinking of Batos or of the present moment in any way. But the moment had found him, and now he had to apologize.

"I am sorry for my lack of sensitivity. I was not referring to you or your . . . " His voice grew quiet, but his mouth still made the shape of a word. "I was thinking aloud about the prophet Daniel and this scroll." Perhaps he should stop here.

Batos nodded gently. "My mother pulled me out of the fire. I was five years old. I was wearing a belt that I had made to carry my knife, and she grabbed it. Lifted me straight up into the air with one hand. I remember hanging above the flames. The heat and the smoke. I didn't feel the burn until later. She set me upright and away from the fire. She said I was polished by the gods." He paused. "That's where the memory ends."

The two horses stopped at a clearing together, as if they wanted to pause to enjoy the view. Between them and the mid-afternoon sun was the main road and then the sea. Virgos pondered the images that Batos had described and the strength of the woman who lifted him out of the fire. Did not the text say "it was she who rescued a righteous man?"

Domitia arrived behind them, and the trio slowed to a stop. She leaned forward and rested the side of her face on the ridge of the mare's mane. She exhaled and let her arms fall. Her hands met underneath the horse's neck. She sat up straight again and took in the view. A buzzard circled high above. Resting on a cushion of air, its flight seemed effortless. Dipping the tip of a wing to turn, the buzzard caught an invisible current of air and rose, only to level out again. Virgos felt his stomach rise with it.

Batos was transfixed. "I thought you might like eagles, since you were in the Roman military," Domitia said, interrupting his reverie.

"Eagles are enlisted like anyone else. Buzzards are their own masters. Lords of life and death," he said, turning toward the trail.

"We'll stop early. There's a good place up here." He gestured with his chin ahead of them. They followed the subtle movement and gathered in a flat, bald place.

Once back on the ground, Virgos felt the ground pushing up beneath the soles of his feet and steadied himself against the horse. He heard voices but could not make out words. From the opposite side of the horse, he thought it might be Batos or Domitia speaking. Walking around the stallion's head, he found them both silent. The voices resumed from far off as indistinct murmurs. "Do you hear that?" Virgos asked.

Domitia stepped away from her saddle. Batos did the same. "Someone is coming," he said. "The two of you can hide in that grove over there. I'll take care of it," he said.

"Wait. I have an idea," Virgos said, imagining the ruse he could create.

"What are you going to do?" Domitia asked."

"I can get rid of them," Virgos said confidently.

Batos did not speak, but his discomfort showed on his face. Domitia shook her head and said "We can help you. And why do you need to do it in the first place?"

Virgos said again, "I can get rid of them."

Batos seemed to decide abruptly. He took the reins of Virgos' horse. "We'll be here. If you need us, call out and we will assist."

Virgos said, "Thank you." He made sure to catch Domitia's eyes with the victory. She held her mouth open in disbelief but did not speak. She followed the others to the grove in silent protest. She pointed to her eye and then to him. He understood her meaning. She would be close, and she would be watching.

Virgos took a lamp, a canteen of water, and a small loaf of bread out of his bag and walked toward the voices. He followed the sound until it became louder and more distinct. He spotted two men walking through the underbrush and called out to them. "Are you looking for an honest man?"

Startled, they struggled to know how to respond. One of them shouted, "What?"

"Are you looking for an honest man?" Virgos repeated. "Your search ends here. Come, sit with me. The body is a heavy load." He beckoned them to come closer and sit together. "Leave the folly of extravagance behind. Simple bread and water for us. We live in accord with nature! Am I right, friends?"

They gathered and sat on fallen logs and a boulder. Virgos spoke calmly to put them at ease. "I am my own king and lord out here," he said. "The conventional life is a trap. Now I am free to live as I please and say what I please. What brings you to the land of freedom?"

One of the men spoke. On the basis of appearance alone, he was the smarter of the two. "We are looking for a woman and a weakling. The woman's name is Domitia."

"Why are you looking for them?" Virgos asked.

"Bracteus' money, that's why," said the second man. "He has all of Pergamum searching for them. Most of the search parties went south, but we went north." He looked at Virgos' long hair and dirty tunic. "Are you one of those Cynicals?"

"I believe you mean 'Cynic,' but both may exist together."

"Whatever," the second man said.

"Have you seen any sign of the woman and the weakling?" Virgos asked.

The first one grunted. "No. You're the first person we've seen. The woman is the one he wants. He said the weakling is disposable."

"Will you eat with me?" Virgos asked. "I have only what the earth has given me, but I will happily share."

Both men nodded. Virgos turned his back to them as he prepared the bread. From the pocket of his tunic, he brought out the alabaster bottle of hellebore he had stolen from Bracteus' desk. He tore the bread in two pieces and poured half of the hellebore liquid on each. Turning to face them, he said, "Please, enjoy. I have flavored the bread with sweet water from Halicarnassus and herbs from Mount Ida."

Each man reached for the bread and stuffed it into their mouths. Crumbs fell to the ground beneath one man. He picked them up and ate them. Virgos watched the poison take effect with a calm, detached curiosity. Uncertain of its specific effects, he was interested to see the outcome. They did not clutch their throats or gaze at him in angry accusation. They simply started to drool and spit yellow liquid at the ground. One of them rubbed his belly, stood up, and fell on his side. He reached out for something in the air. A hallucination, perhaps. The other man vomited twice and fell forward, landing on his forehead, so that the liquid could not escape his mouth. Virgos sat quietly until both of the men lay still.

"What was in the bottle?" asked Domitia from behind him. He did not know that she had left the grove of trees. Batos stood beside her, studying the men intently.

"Hellebore," Virgos said.

"Was it poison?" she asked.

"It could be," he said with a shrug.

"Are they dead?"

Virgos realized that he did not care. "I have no idea."

"If they are not dead now, they will be soon," Batos said. He looked around the clearing and then up at the sun. "We'll leave the bodies here," he said. "We can get in a few hours of travel before dark. If the news is out, if there is a bounty, there will be others."

Virgos stood and picked up his lamp and canteen. The alabaster jar was empty. If there were other search parties or bounty hunters, he would need a different method of defense.

Chapter 13

Domitia

IF SHE MISSED, SHE would have to chase the arrow. She had missed several times already. Traipsing through the bushes looking for arrows was not an efficient way to practice. She stood tall with her left arm straight, and pulled back slow. She brought the string to the center of her mouth. Usually, at this point, her body and mind fused together. Her surroundings seemed irrelevant. But the outside was seeping in, and she could not settle her thoughts.

She released the arrow anyway. It hit a tree, but not the right one. She swore. When she reached the arrow, she yanked it out of the wood and trudged back to camp. Her muscles protested after days of riding. She had washed her face, but she needed a bath. She stunk. She needed to familiarize herself with the outdoor life.

Holding the bow in one hand and the arrow in the other, she found Batos sitting in front of the fire. He was stirring a stew in an iron pot. Absorbed in the process, he stirred, tasted, and then stirred again. He sat up and rested his forearms on his knees when she spoke.

"Aren't you going to tell me what I am doing wrong?" she asked.

"No. You know what you are doing," He stood and walked over to his travel bag. He fished out a small leather bag tied at the top with a drawstring. A mare had returned from wherever she had gone, and he rubbed her neck in a wordless greeting.

"Don't you tie your horses when you set up camp?" Domitia asked without thinking. It was another question that expected him to do something that he was not doing.

"No," he said. "She likes to meander." The mare stepped forward into him, butting his chest with her forehead. He let out an involuntary "oof" and took a step back. "Barbarian," he said wryly, and returned to the fire.

Once in his cooking stance, he pulled at the drawstring of the small pouch. "Cumin!" he said, raising his eyebrows with excitement. He took a pinch between his thumb and index finger and rubbed them together over the pot. He sucked the remainder off his finger and thumb. "Lentils, cumin, the rest of the vegetables . . . I have figs, too, if you want one. Now what I really like is dates, but we don't have any." He sat down the spoon and waited. She must have given him the impression that she wanted to talk. She swore again.

"Did you use a bow in the cavalry?" she asked.

"Yes, but it wasn't my favorite. I prefer a short javelin, if I have a choice. It's lighter, barbed blade, has a strap in the middle of the shaft. Good range. Better control. I have one right over there." He motioned toward his things behind him, talking comfortably. "I used a longer spear, too, but I don't need that very often now. Being left-handed, I had to adjust to whatever was given to me. Throwing was my main weapon. Knife and javelin. That's enough."

She noted the heavy cape of muscles on his left shoulder. "I saw your knife earlier. Is there something carved into the grip?"

He reached around his waist to his belt, grasped his knife, spun it around in his hand with his fingers, and offered her the hilt. She took it from him. "It's a lion's tooth," he said. "I wanted to carve her face, but that was too hard."

Domitia heard the reference to "her", but did not comment. She returned the knife and he put it back in his belt. It was his turn to ask her a question. "Where did you get your bow?" he asked.

"My father had it made. It was probably the best thing he ever did for me. I wanted a Parthian bow, but he refused. He said that the only place for a Parthian was kneeling before Rome on a coin. He found an old man from Thrace to make it. And it is beautiful. It is a work of art. The size is perfect for me. The pull is surprisingly hard, considering how light the wood is. But I like the challenge of it." She felt as if he understood. "I tried a gastraphetes once. It made me nauseous."

"It did the same for me," he said with a soft laugh. "A bulky thing not worth the effort."

The pauses between sentences calmed her. She could speak if she wanted to speak or be silent if she wanted to be silent. She could be content with either.

"My father didn't want me to compete in archery," she said. "It was suitable for visiting ambassadors and demonstrations of local skill. A curiosity. I argued with him about it. Spartan women competed. He said they competed in order to demonstrate their ability to withstand childbirth. I failed at that, so why do it at all? My husband agreed with everything my father said, so I stopped arguing. At least until my husband died."

"I'm sorry that happened to you," Batos said quietly.

"Which thing? Do you mean my husband? It was no loss. I did what I was supposed to do, and so did he. He was vaguely pleased with me, the way you would comment on a new footstool or a wine that you can serve at any occasion." She smoothed her tunic to address the growing tension inside. "Performing like a rich woman. That's all I've ever done. I don't want to do it anymore," she said. The thought was both novel and familiar. "Did you ever marry?" she asked.

"Almost," he said.

"And . . . ?"

"I left home. Raven was her name. Hair the color of a fallen acorn. Quiet in the woods, but not anywhere else. I loved that about her."

Domitia was not sure which thing he loved, but perhaps he meant all of them. It was another ellipse that she may determine someday. He offered her a bowl of stew, and she accepted. Sharing the meal now, they made occasional comments that were not connected to any topic in particular. The stream of consciousness conversation comforted her.

Virgos stirred nearby and woke from a nap. "The smell of deliciousness has roused me," he said with a dramatic flourish, reaching for a bowl. "I fell asleep. I dreamed of the prophet Zechariah. I was the king," he said. He looked at Domitia. "You stood at my right hand. The walls fell, and all the exiles returned."

"You should start writing your dreams down," she said. Virgos agreed through a mouthful. "Maybe the meaning will reveal itself."

He nodded and gestured toward the heavens. "May it be so."

Chapter 14

Batos

in his own words

I'M LYING PRONE, ON my stomach and propped up on my elbows, trying to find the edges of a shadow in the dark. The moon was almost full, which helped. But I had been staring through the hour of twilight and I could not figure out what this animal was.

I'm about three hundred paces out. Pretty close, and they have no idea that I'm there. Just going about their business. Locking animals up for the night, tying their cages shut, stacking cages on top of each other. Traders like these give animals the minimal amount of food and water to keep them alive until they reach the games, wherever the games will be. Animal fights in arenas . . . it's the worst. The lowest form of entertainment. Sick bastards all of them, if you ask me. So I do my part.

These idiots are laughing and shoving each other around, getting ready for their nightly game. They started drinking wine early in the day. They are getting sloppy, which is what I was hoping for. Waiting for them to get sloppy, fall asleep, or slow their reflexes enough to give me time to get in and out with a minimum of collateral damage.

These particular traders were new to the storage part. Hunters maybe, but they were ignorant as far as how to get the animals ready for transport for ships north or other arenas in Mauretania. They kept their animals on the outside of a low wall, outside of the settlement, and unsupervised overnight. If I was lucky, they would do the same as they had every other night for the last week. Check the ropes, gates, and cage latches drunk, preoccupied with the game, and leave them alone through the night. That would give me the perfect opportunity to slip in and do what I do.

But I did not know what this animal was. The shadow kept changing. The other animals I could see, or hear, or smell. Leopards, ostriches, flamingoes, pigs, and a mystery animal. A little helmethead gecko was sitting there with me, watching, and I say, "Do you know what that is?" He swirls away, all toes and tail. On the way to my scouting point, I had seen elephant tracks heading the other direction. One bull, solo, moving fast. Probably escaped and on his way home.

This shadow was like a triangle with two little triangle shapes on top. The whole thing was on top of a pole. Ears, I guessed. Does it hear me? About the height of a tall person. Head was too big to be an ostrich. Too tall to be a gazelle. Horns weren't long enough. The lower edge of the triangle rises and falls. Then a lurch, a movement in jerky starts and stops, and a rise into the air that keeps going and going. The lower edge becomes a jawline, the pole becomes a neck until it towers over all the other animals. That clears it up. It's a giraffe, and the giraffe had been lying down. Dangerous hooves. Can knock you flat from front or back. Fast runner. Now I know what I'm dealing with and can plan my route.

I'll open the cages of the quiet animals first. Sometimes the quiet ones are the most dangerous. Ideally, they can get away, and they won't kill each other or me. I'll start with the leopards and let them run. Then the ostriches and flamingoes. Flamingoes can be loud, but sometimes they just mill around and need to be convinced. While they're deciding whether or not to escape, I can cut the capture nets for the lions and whatever ropes laying around. The giraffe could come next. Finally, the pen of pigs. These were not bound for the games. They are for eating. That gate should be easy to open, but pigs can squeal in unison and rouse the dead. And they can be mean.

But I have my route. Idiots have started their game, completely oblivious. Now is the time. My knife is sharp. I am ready.

Chapter 15

Virgos

The Attack

"Ho, everyone who thirsts, come to the waters. Come, drink, without pay," Virgos said to himself. The other two were not listening. "That's good because I don't have any money, and no one is going to pay me. The Spirit of the Lord God is upon me, not them. He has sent me to bind up the brokenhearted and to refill the canteens of my fellow travelers." He often said things for the subtle intertextual joy of it. Isaiah would not object.

Truth be told, he had run out of water and did not mind the excursion. Another day of riding had come and gone. He ached, but the trio had become accustomed to the daily rhythms of travel. Now out of sight of Batos and Domitia, he could listen to the scriptures in his mind uninterrupted and imagine what they might say to one another. Wisdom had become a companion for Isaiah on topics that mattered a great deal to him. What would it be like to host a symposium and invite the prophets, such as Isaiah, Daniel, Zechariah, Ezekiel, and the author of Wisdom, whoever that might be? Add now these two new figures, Paul of Tarsus and Jesus of Nazareth. About them he knew only scraps and anecdotes and remnants of others' stories. Domitia had told him about the letter from Julia Severa. The promise of a Messiah is fulfilled in a crucified criminal! What a marvel and stumbling block that would be. The play in Pergamum had shown them a glimpse of that as well. And what did the director of the theater troupe say before the play began? "Jesus who takes on the sin of the world." Invite them all and seat them together. Would this symposium erupt in laughter and companionship, or would they tear each other apart? He could imagine no greater joy of just being there, being with them.

There was no path down to the stream. He descended into the ravine carefully but enjoyed the creativity of making up a route. He ducked under a low hanging branch and stood up on the other side. "Take that, Absalom," he said, smoothing his hair. The water gave a small bubbling welcome. The stream had taken the time to curve around a tree, form a small island, and meet on the other side. Hardly the Jabbok, but water nonetheless. He might find some wood for the fire as well. A broom tree perhaps.

At the edge of the water, he balanced on one stone, and then another. The stones rocked back and forth in a deep melody but held firm. He leapt to the shore on the other side and landed softly in the mud. On this side, the incline of the ravine was steep and gave little room to walk. He knelt at the water and reached for it.

He saw a great light and felt a warm sensation at the back of his head. Thick liquid behind his ear. Pain from the back of his head toward the front. Sweet mud in his mouth and cool water on his face. A wet rock touching the temple. A violent yank upwards and backwards.

He saw the gleam of a knife and felt hands force him to his knees. The hands held him down so that he could not rise. He twisted and saw three men behind him. One held a tree branch and one held a knife. The other stood and watched. As he twisted, he felt the edge of the knife on his jaw. Was that a kneecap in his spine? He heard the crunch of bone on bone and felt his vertebrae separate. One of his knees slid down the incline as he fought, but he could not free himself from their grip.

"Shear him like a sheep," one man said.

"This is the eunuch we were looking for. Cut him bare. Down to the skin," another said.

He tried to stand but was pulled down again. Flailing with a stone in his hand, he heard one blow collide with forehead. No. You will not take my hair. But the force and the spinning were too much. He saw a scrap of curtain the color of his hair falling. It landed softly on the pine needles below. A feather.

A flurry of movement passed in front of him. He heard an arrow enter one of the thugs in the abdomen. The air closed behind the arrow as if the air had never been disturbed. On his right, the body of the man holding the tree branch fell limp over the arrow. On his left, the body of the man with the knife fell. This one had a spear in his ribs. The spear had been thrown with tremendous power.

Virgos fell onto his back on the steep incline. Ah gentle bed. He saw Domitia's face above him. Her mouth was moving, but he heard only wordless growls. Elisha, your she-bear has come. Her voice broke through the din. She said his name. "I am a dying Gaul!" he said to her, but her face clouded.

"How many?" Batos asked. "How many were there?"

"Three," Virgos said. "There were three."

Virgos looked at the scaffold of trees above him. The wind lifted the leaves and made the needles whistle. His friends helped him to his feet. As he stood, he grasped the clump of his hair from the ground and brought it close to his face. "Bald head! Bald head!" he shouted.

He felt their shoulders in his armpits as they moved him forward. They stepped across the stream and up the other side of the ravine. His mouth was making too much saliva. His thoughts were not aligned. He compressed the panic of not knowing.

He thought of Carmel, of Sinai, of Nebo. I will remember, Lord. You delivered me from those who hated me. Your strong arms lifted me from the valley of death. I will rebuild your altar. I will serve you all my days.

Chapter 16

Domitia

The Attack

A SHARP CRACK OF sound turned her head toward the ravine. Was that a tree branch falling? Domitia listened carefully. Virgos had gone down to the stream and had not returned. She heard a guttural sound of defiance and voices she did not recognize. "Did you hear that?" she asked Batos. He had been even farther away from the sound, repairing a leather strap.

But Batos was already moving toward the sound. She saw only his back and a javelin in his hand. He moved like a cat unleashing its coiled energy, leaping over the fire one foot at a time. He plunged over the edge of the ravine and out of sight.

She grabbed her bow and the only arrow she had. Why didn't she retrieve the ones she had been using for practice? It was only the briefest of regrets, and then a calm flowed over her. One is all I need. Resolved, she crested the rim of the ravine and raced down, looking for Virgos. She saw him on the far side of the stream. He was down on one knee, facing her, with the other leg extending out to one side. One man stood behind him sawing at his hair with a knife, and the other man held him down. Wildly swinging his arms, mouth full of blood, Virgos was locked in violent battle like the son of Gaia on the Great Altar. He was a Titan struggling to break free, and she was his mother, sister, friend. She watched with horror but could not get there quickly enough to stop it from ever happening. It was already happening, and she had to get there now.

She had not been trained to shoot at a moving target while moving, and she had to adapt in an instant. Sliding down the stony hill, she focused on the man behind Virgos. The one doing the sawing. She would have to be precise because Virgos was directly in front of him. If the man stepped to her left, she would have an opening. She found a rock ledge that would hold. On cue, he stepped to the left, giving her a direct line to the abdomen. I can see you now. She drew back and released. The arrow found a path through the trees and into his belly. His belly separated with a dull wet sound.

Satisfied, she sprinted forward through the wet stream, into the muddy edge, and up the other side. Virgos was lying on the incline, head raised, rambling about bears. He said something about dying. She snapped at him out of fear. "You are not dying!" she said.

Confident now that Virgos was alive and would recover, she turned her attention to the man she had killed. The arrow had split his belly in the center. It was a good shot. She cocked her head to one side to watch him take his last breath. She raised her leather boot to his shoulder and shoved him. The arrow had propped him up on his side, and he was unable to roll over on his back. She knelt in front of him and leaned forward so that her face was close to his. 'Where are you going?" she asked him. His eyes seemed to pull inward. "Down, down," she sang softly, as she stood up and turned toward Virgos.

She saw bone, scalp, and gristle all tangled together. His hair hung in clumps. She reached for his shoulder to steady him and tried to gauge how deep the wounds were. "I don't know what this is," she said to Batos. "Is this skull?"

Batos' voice was firm. "We'll look at it. Let's get him up and out." As they carried him up the other side of the ravine to camp, he seemed to fade in and out. Present one instant and absent the next. They helped him lay down and rest near his scroll case. His tunic was torn in the back. Watching his breathing, she sat cross-legged next to him and laid a horse blanket over his legs. She asked him "Do you want me to trim it, so that it is even?"

"Not. One. Hair." Virgos responded.

She immediately regretted her question. "I'm sorry." He raised his hand so that his palm faced her. Frustrated with herself, she stood and asked Batos for his knife.

"Why do you want my knife?" he asked.

"I will be right here the entire time, and I will give it back," she said impatiently. Batos handed it to her as he had earlier, spinning it with one hand and extending the hilt. She took it and returned to her place at Virgos' side. She sat and pulled her bow into her lap. One line at a time, she carved letters into the grip. Turning the bow at the necessary angles, she formed the letters into a new name. The letters read K-A-I-N.

Darkness had come, and she could no longer see the letters clearly. She wanted to say something to comfort Virgos, but she had already said too much. As her tension subsided, she sat in silence next to him and allowed herself to rest. She felt as if a latch inside her had broken open, and a dove had burst out, flapping noisily toward the sky.

Chapter 17

Batos

The Attack

WHAT HE HAD SEEN that morning was still vivid in his mind. The kingfisher and its killer. Now, near the end of the day, his body was spent, but his mind was not.

This morning, he had been sitting in his usual way up against a young pine. He pulled his knees up to his chest and rested his forearms on his knees. He watched the day open in this way. It was a habit he started when he worked Last Watch. The small animals emerged and talked to one another. It was still cool at this time in the mountains. He savored the transition from night to day. Some were waking up. Others were going to their rest.

He was watching a kingfisher bird perched at the end of a fallen log. The log extended across a tiny sliver of fresh water and a small eddy on the far side of the bank. The bird called out to another bird, who responded. Suddenly, he stabbed the water. He emerged with a fish in his beak. Water dripped from the end of the wriggling thing. He held on with a talon-like grip. He opened his throat and swallowed it whole in two gulps.

As the bird swallowed, a shape moved behind him. The other creature moved quickly and silently. Three steps at a time, groups of three in succession behind the bird. It was a marten. Claws flashed white on the tree bark as he crept toward a catch of his own. Batos opened his mouth to warn the bird, but the death blow happened so quickly that he did not have time. The marten flashed four canine teeth. Batos heard the snap of bone and saw the odd angle of the bird's broken neck dangling from the marten's mouth. Feet and feathers dangled loosely above the bark. Turning toward Batos, the marten looked directly at him. It was an intimacy he was unprepared for. Then the marten slipped into the undergrowth.

Why didn't the bird hear him? Why didn't the bird turn around? After a day's worth of thought, the questions remained unanswered. In the meantime, in the current moment, other issues pressed for attention. The breast collar for his saddle needed repair. He could not find the small piece of rope that could piece it together until they reached Assos. The stable there would have what he needed.

Virgos had gone down to the water. He had looked up from his scroll and announced it. Virgos thought no one heard or appreciated his humor, but that was not the case.

Batos heard a crack of wood and a small splash. The crack sounded like wood breaking, but the disturbance of water was a fall. The sounds came from a lower point in the earth, possibly from the water at the center of the ravine. In an instant, he was up and moving toward it. He grasped his javelin with one hand. He heard a cry. Springing forward and then down over the ridge, he saw the route open up before him. Leaping off of one foot, with his chest forward, he oriented himself in the air. His left shoulder reached back into the farthest point of his range. He fired and watched the javelin fly true. He landed on the other side of the boulder, farther down the descent, and kept moving down the hill. In the space of a step, he had lifted his knife from his belt and held it ready.

Off to his left, he saw Domitia moving instinctively to the left wing while he took the right. Two men held Virgos down. One was cutting his hair and his face, and the other held him by the shoulders. She was in a good position to take the one on the left, and she had just fired. He saw his own javelin land between two ribs. Two men down. There may be more.

He crossed the water and reached the men. Confident that his javelin had hit the mark, he finished the man off anyway. In the interest of efficiency, he made one quick stab into the fold between the pelvis and the thigh. An underestimated location. He pulled the javelin out of the man's chest, looking around but still assessing what was in front of him. Virgos had done some damage to this one. His forehead had a dent in it. He saw Domitia kneeling in front of the dying man she had shot. From the look on her face, he was worried she might get a taste for it. He said her name twice, but she did not respond. Was she smiling? He needed her to pull out and engage.

Virgos had been beaten badly, but he was alive. Scrapes and slices covered his face. He ear was either missing or covered in blood. Blood was dripping from the back of his skull down his spine. Other wounds would reveal themselves in time. Lying on his back on the incline of the ravine, he was muttering the prophets. He held a clump of hair in his hand.

"How many?" asked Batos. "How many were there?"

"Three," Virgos said clearly. "There were three."

Batos scanned the ravine but saw only two. Had one gotten away? Were there three at all? He could return later to see what he could see in the dark. Tracks, perhaps, or slips of feet on the steep trail. "Let's get him up and out," he said to Domitia. This time she had heard him, but she was focused on Virgos. She looked stricken. He could not decide if she was going to vomit or go back to the dead man's body and shoot it again.

They stepped to either side of him, lifted him by the torso, and placed each of his arms over their shoulders. From up close, he could see that a portion of Virgos' ear was missing. He thought of the lion in his dream who had suffered the same. Virgos turned to him. His head wobbled but his gaze was intentional. "Bears," Virgos said.

Batos considered saying, "Actually, I was thinking about a lion." But he chose not to confuse the matter further. "We are taking you to camp. It's over now. Now you can rest." Domitia posted herself by his side as they settled near the fire. She watched him with the eyes of a raptor bird. She would watch him carefully. Of that he had no doubt. An inn was up ahead, on the main road to the north and west, but a manageable distance. He could go there for wine and balm for wounds, if they had any. Twilight was here, and darkness would soon follow. But he did not mind walking in the dark.

Chapter 18

Domitia

"I AM MAKING SURE you are alive," Domitia said to Virgos. "That's why I'm staring." Sitting next to a small fire, Virgos was beginning to return to himself. He washed his wounds with water she had brought up for him. Batos had found no balm on his night venture, but he did find another tunic, a round of barley bread, and a jug of wine. The jug had been heavy when he arrived. Now it was nearly empty.

The wine had soothed her and brought some relief to the raw edges caused by the attack. Slurred speech was its own kind of comfort. Each of them had drank enough to reach that point, and not one of them was troubled by it. She looked at the two of them in the firelight, one at a time. She was one of three. A rogue triumvirate, free to go where they pleased.

"If we were in Pergamum, someone would make a speech," Domitia said. "An encomium would be appropriate," she said.

Virgos responded with a shout. He closed his eyes as if the thought had delighted him. "Yes! Let the speeches begin." Batos raised a cup and agreed.

Domitia stood, raised her cup of wine in the air, and asked, "To whom shall I express my gratitude? The emperor Claudius?"

Batos shook his head. "Claudius isn't as bad as the one before him. Now Caligula, there's one who needs a tribute." She took a dramatic breath and began.

"An encomium, from the horse Incitatus, to the Emperor Caligula, affectionately known (to the horse) as Big Booties." Virgos and Batos clapped and leaned forward with anticipation. "Oh Big Booties, the glory is yours. I bring praise and gratitude to you today for the many privileges you have showered upon me both at home and abroad. Your modesty and relentless pursuit of moderation provided for me a stall made of marble, paved trails, gold shoes encrusted with precious stones, and grain grown in the warm light of Numidia. A fountain runs with fresh water, and my baths are warm and regular. For the races, you gave me and my friends frog green colors. You provided me with a doctor, a priest, a tailor, and legal assistance against my adversary Manurra. Fine humans from the auxiliary cavalry tended to my daily needs."

Batos interjected, "That's right!"

"You honored me," she continued, "with the privilege of escorting you across the sea, jumping effortlessly from boat to boat across the bay from Baiae to Puteoli. You staged a victory over the sea, and we returned dressed in the finest gold cloaks and purple crowns. As a display of your bodily excellence, health, and strength, you danced for us. Even though our hooves do not clap together like those of people, your great knowledge knew that we were clapping, and you bowed." Domitia leaned forward and whispered, "He can read minds."

"I acknowledge that stories will be written about me and this occasion of victory, thus described, that brought me the title of Maximus Equus. In imitation of you and your reluctance to accept honors, I declined the title at first. Out of your magnanimity, you persuaded me to accept it. Acceptance seemed fitting if only to reflect the greatness of your company. Seeking that generosity now, I ask for small favors. I ask that renovations of the stables and barns might continue, so that your equine companions might receive the honors that are due to them. Projects that reflect your magnificence and munificence should be carried out with the most expedience. With full awareness that the immortal gods will not hear me, I vow to the immortal gods anyway for your health and safety and well-being. We raise a hoof to you, Big Booties, and praise your name forever."

"Amen," Virgos said. Both he and Batos shaped their hands like horse hooves and made hollow clapping sounds. Domitia sat down and drained the wine in her cup.

Virgos said thoughtfully, "I do believe I am intemperant."

"You are yourself again. You are saying things that sound like they were written long ago," Domitia said. "Would you like to make a speech?"

Virgos stood and began, "Be it resolved. Therefore, heretofore, I will demonstrate. I will cast caution aside and craft an impious farce." Domitia and Batos rubbed their hands together, eager for the show. "I will set the scene for you. Imagine. A parade approaches in Rome. Not a mere parade, but an ovation. We are fortunate, blessed beyond recognition, to be present tonight at a triumphant procession of losers. Brutes, boors, feminine foreigners and soft suckers, all counted as booty for Caligula's victory at Puteoli. Leading the parade is General Eirene. She rides a horse named Hegemony—er, Harmony—and proclaims the good news of victory over the sea."

"Seated on a high stage, dressed as gods, the emperor Gaius Caesar Germanicus, known to some as Caligula, and his entourage take in the spectacle. His face is painted red, and he wears a purple toga. As each trophy parades in front of him, he lowers his scepter toward it and grants it the privilege of staying alive for the duration of the ovation. Next to the emperor sits a buzzard on a metal stand. (The eagle was not available. He had flown to greet the prophet Isaiah and did not return.) A slave stands behind the emperor on the left. He was told to hold a crown directly above the emperor's head, but he resists. He holds the crown above the buzzard's head instead. Intoxicated by the splendor before him, the emperor does not notice. Another slave stands behind the emperor on the right. She was told to hold a wax image of Augustus, but she resists. She holds the image close to a lamp instead. The wax melts so that the features of Augustus are unrecognizable."

"The ovation commences with a grand flourish. General Eirene leads a group of emperors who no longer sit on the throne. Each is wearing his finest toga. Some have wings. Some tied their hands to a stone so that they would not float away. Some are wearing name tags. The general calls out to the crowd: "Repeat after me! Gaius is a god!"

The crowd shouts back, "Gaius is a goose!"

The general attempts to correct them. "No. I said, 'Gaius is a god!"

The crowd shouts back, "Gaius is a goose!" The group of emperors stop in front of the stage and bow in unison, but they bow the opposite direction. Again, lost in a fugue of glory, the emperor does not notice. Now it's time for the choir. Each member of the choir carries a chamber pot filled with the remains of the vanquished. They too stop in front of the emperor's stage. The director raises his arms and they hit a shrill, dissonant note. A screech of discord. They simultaneously dump the contents of their pots, singing as they do it. The emperor raises his arms to pull the scent toward him. Victory smells sweet."

"As the ovation ends, the emperor stands. "Thank you, my subjects. Your admiration is warranted. With your praise to lift me, I have ascended to great heights. From this divine post, I can see both the resources you represent and the opportunities I have to utilize them. With great joy in my heart, I will dance for you!" He bursts into a frenzied staccato of movement, and the crowd erupts in applause."

With wild uncoordinated abandon, Virgos began to dance himself. Domitia and Batos shouted words of acclamation. Virgos bowed in the opposite direction and sat down with a smile. They sat together with the images he had created. He said to Batos, "Your turn."

"I don't do plays, but I'll do this," he said. He stood and raised one arm straight out to his side. Pointing toward the west, he said nothing. He stood quietly with his face composed. Domitia waited for him to say something, but he did not.

"What are you?" she asked.

"I'm a sign," said Batos.

"A sign of what?" asked Virgos.

"Just a sign. 'This way for a good time. Ask for Claudius.'"

Domitia said, "Not Caligula? What do you have to say about him?"

Batos sat and stretched his legs out in front of him. He placed both hands on his boots. "Very little," he said.

All three laughed and raised their cups to one another. They settled into the joyful silence. Domitia was grateful. If only for a while, Virgos' pain had subsided. She could barely remember a time when she had not known Batos. It was as if he had always been there. He had found no tracks of a third man, but that would wait until tomorrow. They would face whatever came together.

Chapter 19

Virgos

ONLY WITH GREAT EFFORT could he gather his faculties. The top of his head felt separate from the rest of his body. He could not decide if it was the injury or the wine. Pulling himself slowly to a sitting position, he gingerly touched the wounds on the back of his head. The jug lay empty next to Domitia, who was sleeping deeply on the far side of the embers. He heard footsteps, and turned to see Batos approaching. He had never seen Batos sleep.

"Figs?" Batos asked. He sat down and fished through the food bag. It was almost empty. Virgos accepted a fig and chewed with a new awareness of the muscles in his jaw. Batos spoke softly. "Have you had to deal with morons like that your whole life?"

"I didn't castrate myself, if that's what you mean. 'Eunuch' is a title others give to me. I was born with one where there are normally two. All else is assumption."

Batos nodded and made a thoughtful sound. The quiet between them was an open door, and Virgos decided to walk through it.

"I want to hurt them," Virgos said. He felt a searing at his center. Is this what the truth felt like?

"We did hurt them," Batos said.

"Not those thugs. All of them."

Batos' voice was firm. "Their days are numbered."

Virgos was not comforted. "But my anger—my anger—cannot reach them. I see their faces, the disgust, and the bond that disgust forms among them. The private became public, and it can never go back again.

"I was discovered to be deficient in the baths. I snuck in with friends as a boy. I did not think they would ridicule me for it. My parents had told me to avoid the baths, but I thought my friends would either not notice or not care. I was wrong. They told me I should come to the baths on Ladies Day. They said that I was fortunate to be alive. Most parents would have exposed me.

"My father was furious. 'I told you to stay away from the baths,' he said. He and my mother had been cast out of Rome when Tiberius expelled the Jews, and they started a new life in Pergamum. They moved to a new city, had children, and buried their Judaism. When I was born, my body was another thing they had to hide. I argued with my father that I was included in the covenant. He had not read the texts that I had read. There should be no shame, I said, but he would not listen. He just shouted. 'Rome didn't want us, and Jerusalem doesn't want you!'

"My goal then was to become something other than an embarrassment. To outgrow my body. But shame is a meaty thing. The insults stayed the same. There is a startling lack of creativity in that area. I would have respected anyone who could create a nickname that I had not heard. A 'one-man woman,' perhaps." Virgos smiled at his own clever turn of phrase. "But they did not have the mind for it. The title of 'eunuch' became my name."

Virgos felt his fury rise. "The stupid masses don't care if their titles are unimaginative. They don't comprehend the words they eat. They open their mouths like baby birds. Feed me with your standards and your contempt for others. I give you my open gullet. Am I to be grateful that my parents allowed me to live?" Virgos gestured to his groin. "This empty Cynic's wallet is the opposite of freedom."

Virgos took a deep breath and reset his shoulders. "But what if? What if the breath of God stirred the waters and we were unbound by these titles? Each one of us odd and wonderfully made. All sewn together into the covenant. This scroll I carry with me, frayed memories of texts that speak in concord with it, the prophets who see beyond . . . I can stand among these stories. I am not forced to bow.

"But is there a place on this earth where I can stand upright? A place where idols and money and body do not determine membership? A shared commitment to step under each other rather than over? Are these things beyond our grasp?" Virgos asked with a genuine desire to know. "If there is no such place, how do I stop hoping for it?"

Batos had been listening to every word. He said, "I don't think we do."

Virgos coughed up the grief that had gathered in his throat. He touched his head wounds with the tips of his fingers and traced the slices of flesh from the knife's edge across his cheek. Some of his beard had withstood the blade. It would grow again.

Chapter 20

Batos

BATOS LAID HIS HEAD back against the bark of the oak. In his usual watch position, he listened to the night. After wine and laughter, his companions had given themselves over to rest. All angles and corners and straight lines, Virgos slept on his side, with his scroll case tucked under one arm. It was as if he had been made with a plumb line. He had a fierce and confident mind, but he was unaware of his own physical power. Someday the two would meet. Domitia had resisted sleep until she decided that Virgos would heal. His protector and sibling, she was a hunter who had not been allowed to hunt. Restrained, kept, she held her elbows close. But in sleep, her arms were flung straight out to either side.

Batos felt the edges of the bark behind his head and looked up at the branch above. A cicada lifted his wings to cool off. He shook his wings, making a rattling percussive sound, and folded them in again. Suspended under the branch, a leaf fluttered on its short stem. The nubs of the leaf lengthened and became fingers, and the leaf became a hand. It reached down to him, and the branch creaked as it followed. The wood stretched and leaned until the leafy hand approached Batos' hand. He reached out to meet it and placed his hand in it. He saw its veins and felt its green grip.

The branch lifted him to his feet and then up into the air, up through the canopy of pine and oak. At the farthest point of its reach, the branch separated from the tree and rose above the others. He looked up and he saw a smear of dark red blood on the bark above his hand. Below him was the coastal scrub and then the sea. They were flying south. They crossed the blue of the sea and then the green of the plateaus and the ocher and amber of desert. There was no pain and no fear. He felt only flight over the turquoise blue and the giants who live within it. Flight over a land he had spent a lifetime learning, the contours of Mauretania and Numidia, and the grazing grounds of countless herds. A land of steep cliffs and wide plateaus and salty lake beds. Roman roads had dissected the bodies of the plains, and grids had cut it into squares. Each square was marked with a language that the creatures did not recognize.

The branch began to slow and descend. He hovered in the air over the wide stone road laid by the Romans from Tacapae to Ammaedara. Lowering him to his feet, the leaf hand did not let go. His feet rested on the ground lightly next to an ancient cypress. The air smelled of cinnamon and myrrh. On the banks of the road grew cedar, iris, mallow and thyme. The tamarisk was blooming. He saw that the soil under the stones of the road had been measured and scraped to make the road level. The stones were laid flat for wheels and boots of marching infantry. In the vast horizon, from the west to the east, he could not see where the road began or ended. In the center of the road was a large Roman tent made of skin.

He listened and he heard water under the road. The water began to rumble and roar. It seeped through the cracks between the stones and bubbled up in the spaces where the corners met. Gathering its strength, the water erupted in high fountains with the sounds of thunder.

On the banks of the road stood all the animals of the deserts and mountains and forests. The animals who slept under the sand awoke. They watched the water and the tent. A great chasm opened, loosening the stones so that the tent began to fall. The pegs broke free and the tent fell, from the center to the edge, disappearing into the water below. One by one, the stones fell. The markers fell. The tent was no more.

And the plants and animals bore witness. Each spoke of resistance, each in their own language. The plants did not hold their ground around the tent pegs. Trees bore fruit that would not ripen. Corn refused to pay tribute. Caracal, fox, and horned viper. Panther, ox, and broad-backed dog all stood by the side of the road. They did not rescue the tent. They stood silently as the tent and the road and all its people were swallowed by the earth. A horse stood nearby. She had been burned with a hot iron. The mark said "LegIII." She turned and walked into the desert.

Batos stood among the animals and the plants. With them he heard a voice coming up from the water under the tent. "Their days are numbered. Jesus of Nazareth, my Anointed One, will rise. He will climb up from the pit of Sheol, and he will offer you everlasting life. A hope beyond this day and a wisdom beyond this age." After the voice had spoken, roots emerged from the earth. They had signaled to one another in the dark and rose up into the light. "This is the day that the Lord has made," said the voice. "This is the day that the Lord made you. Speak your language. Say your name."

The branch lifted Batos into the air. He looked and he saw no stones, no markers, and no tents. There was no more road. The branch carried him over the water and all its creatures, The wind brought him across the sea to the oak tree and the smell of smoke.

Batos came back to the present as if pulled by his belly cord. He heard the blow of a horse exhale and the clear whistle of a night bird. The oak tree stood as it had before. The leaf hand fluttered slightly on its stem. Two travelers. Three horses. All accounted for. Supplies running low. Girth needs repair but it will hold until we get to Assos.

He stood up near the remains of the fire and stretched. A finger of cloud hid the waxing moon. He could see a shadow of himself in the remaining light. Returning to his seat, he looked up at the oak tree and wondered if it would reach out to him. He realized that he was sitting on top of a tree root that had emerged from the earth. He decided to sit near it instead.

Chapter 21

Virgos

"How BEAUTIFUL ARE THE feet! And the face! And everything else!" A woman shouted down at them from a second story window.

Surprised by the reference, Virgos shouted in return, "That is Isaiah!" She was wearing an indigo turban and matching caftan. They had arrived in Adramyttium, and Batos had brought them to a shop with an apartment above. Standing at the door of the shop, Batos had knocked and called out a greeting. She suddenly appeared at the window above them and exclaimed with joy.

"Jesus is Lord! Batos has returned!" she said with her head leaning out above them. She disappeared briefly, and Virgos heard her speaking inside the house. "Batos is here!" She appeared again. "Our door is broken. We must use the basket. Apologies to our dear guests, but I must confess. It is an entertaining inconvenience. One moment, please."

As they waited for her to return, Virgos and Domitia peered into the window of the shop on the first floor. It was closed for business, but he could see hundreds of funeral urns. Two ossuaries sat next to one another along the far wall. A pithos burial jar stood in the back corner, and a long workbench was built into the wall next to it. He wondered what kind of house this was, and what awaited them above. The woman above might be in the business of death, but she may also be, to an equal degree, in the business of life after death.

She leaned out of the window again, this time with two men. The three of them lowered a large woven basket made of leather and fabric strips. Tall enough for a person to stand in, the basket had a heavy rope tied to either side. They lowered it down from the window until it reached the ground. "Step in, Batos! You first. We will raise you up."

Batos stifled a laugh, threw one leg over the side, and stood in the center of the basket. He looked up at them as they lifted the basket off the ground. The ropes rubbed against the window ledge as they pulled the basket up. At the base of the window, they took his hands and he leapt in. They embraced one another and stepped away from the window. A deep laugh echoed from inside the house. The sound drifted down to them as they looked up toward the open window. He thought it might be Batos, but Virgos had never heard him laugh before. The door of the shop opened, and one of the basket men appeared before them. "Our door is working now." It had made no unusual sound, and showed no sign that it was broken. "Please, come in," he said.

Once inside the house, Virgos took in the joy that surrounded them. It was like balm to his wounds. The small rooms were full of people milling about, carrying on multiple conversations at once. Batos was clearly a beloved figure. "Our handsome vision has returned," someone said to him. "Come, sit by me. It has been too long." He seemed sheepish at the attention but greeted each person intentionally. The woman in the turban escorted them to a living room with three couches and a single chair on the far wall. Food and wine were arranged on a table in the middle, offered freely, and passed around the room. Painted in Greek on the wall behind the chair, in a semi-circle, was the phrase "A Prophet Has Arisen." Graffiti covered the space around it. In a myriad of languages, visitors had written the names of prophets or excerpts from holy texts on the wall. Some of the languages he had never seen, but he could read and grasp most of the names and titles. Someone had written the name of Batos in Greek next to the name of Daniel in Hebrew. Titles were written on top of one another: Messiah, Christ, Savior, Anointed One, Son of Man, Son of God. The word "Love" was written in Greek and Latin next to the drawing of a wooden cross.

"My name is Pteleah," she said to Virgos, "but you can call me Leah. And your name?"

"Virgos," he said. He was struck by the calm and magnetic energy she radiated. He did not want to look anywhere else.

"Welcome. And your name?" she asked Domitia.

"My name is Kaineus," she said. Virgos pondered the change but said nothing. He remembered her carving letters into her bow. K-A-I-N, the letters had read. She was not naming her bow. She was naming herself, and the carving was not yet completed. A reference to Ovid, perhaps, and his poem of transformation. Or perhaps she had been changed by the act of crossing the stream and killing a man on the other side.

"Welcome, Kaineus. Find a seat anywhere you like. Introduce yourself. There are no strangers here."

Kaineus touched her own forehead, drawing attention to a luminous beryl stone attached to the knot of Leah's turban. "What a lovely stone," she said.

"Do you like it?" said Leah. "It was a gift from Batos." A crashing sound interrupted her. It sounded like the shattering of glass. "One moment, my dears." As she glided away, Virgos noticed that her slippers matched her caftan and turban. From the other room, he heard Leah say firmly, "Attis and Adonis. Cabbage is not a weapon. Put it down." After a brief pause, Leah returned, glowing and composed. She held her arms wide with welcome as she approached her chair.

The two guests were still standing awkwardly, looking around for a place to sit. They squeezed together into a space on one of the couches. A woman walked by and said to them, "That couch is where we put the dead." He could not decide if the woman was teasing him or telling him to use caution. All the guests were serving themselves. Thirsty from the journey, Virgos reached for a cup and filled it with wine from the krater. The wine was sweet and mellow. An expensive vintage, he thought. He had not tasted wine of that quality for some time. A woman with no hair and a scar above one eyebrow approached him and leaned down directly in front of his face. Holding a small clay jar of ointment, she stared intently at his wounds. He was confused by the attention.

"May I?" the woman asked, raising the ointment jar. He agreed, and she gently applied ointment to his wounds. Her hand was gentle but steady.

"What is in it?" he asked.

"Rose oil and resin," she said. She finished her application and squeezed next to him on the couch.

"Myrina is our physician," Leah said from her chair across the room. Virgos nodded and smiled at both of them but did not know what to say. "Our friend Alexander just returned from seeing a satyr play in Lampsacus," Leah said loudly. Her voice carried effortlessly and clearly through the air. She gestured to a young man on the opposite couch.

"That satyr play was hilarious," the young man said. "A new work by Atomia and her troupe. Priapus falls in love with Circe, and all manner of comedy ensues. The rumor in the audience was that the character of Priapus was based on an olive oil merchant from Pergamum."

Kaineus sat up straight. "Did you happen to hear the name of the merchant?"

"Only in passing," Alexander said. "Brateus, maybe?"

Virgos choked on a date. "Bracteus," Kaineus said, pronouncing the "c" in the name.

"Yes, that's it," he said. "Of course, every play that Atomia writes is good. But her plays get better and better. And she gets rich people to pay for them!"

Leah appeared before Virgos and leaned over. "Would you mind getting us some more wine? There should be a small amphora in the basement." Eager to participate in some way, he stood and moved toward the stairs. He followed the narrow stairs down until he reached a dirt floor. He could turn either left or right. He chose the left and entered the room through a low stone arch. Two lamps were lit in one corner. This was clearly the columbarium. Stretched out on the floor was a woman dressed in fine fabrics. She was wearing an elaborate headdress with pearls woven into her braids and a Greek armband with a garnet set in the center. She was lying completely still, with her arms crossed across her chest. In the low light, he could not determine if the woman was alive or dead. Her color could have indicated either one. He backed out slowly and entered the other room. There was the wine jug, just as Leah had said. He sprinted up the stairs, two at a time, and reached the dining room just as Leah was calling everyone to attention.

"Everyone? Your attention please." The chatter subsided and they turned to face her. "Our storyteller has come. Batos, do you have a story to tell us?" He stepped into the center of the room. "It is time for The Story!" Leah shouted.

The room filled with cheers and acclamation. "The Story! We are ready!"

Chapter 22

Batos

LEAH SAT ON THE forward edge of her chair, and the room fell silent. "Welcome to all! We gather in the name of Jesus of Nazareth. We are a creative house. His Story is embodied and performed and lived in this house. For those of you joining us for the first time, we speak when we feel moved to speak. We interact and respond from every seat in the house. We call out, affirm, and add meaning. Let the Story evolve in the moment. For those of us not joining us for the first time, you remember our friend Batos!" A warm chorus of voices swelled. "We begin," her voice rose as she called to the group. "Wisdom has built her house."

"We are the pillars of her house," the group responded in unison.

"The Story I bring to you today has never been performed before," Batos said, turning to speak to everyone from the center of the room. "Somewhere between Troas and Pergamum, this play was born. I saw it develop with my own eyes. The goal was to perform it in Priene. It's an animal fable. I convinced them to write a play about animals because humans assume that the love of God is for them. Love is much bigger than that."

Voices rose from around the room as three members of the group responded.

"The righteous care for the needs of their animals."

"The mountains and the hills will break forth in singing."

"Did you have a role? Did you rehearse with them?"

"No," Batos said. "I was the audience. All of it. The play starts with an actor dressed as a scorpion. He has this tail that won't stand up, even though it is supposed to. It drags behind him. He carries a podium out to the center of the performance area. They didn't have a stage then. He sets it down and makes sure it is in the right spot. Then he walks away. Another actor comes out dressed as Emperor Augustus. He stands in front of a huge arch made out of boards nailed together. The boards are painted to look like marble."

A man near Virgos raised his voice. "That would be a challenge to build, even for us."

"Augustus is wearing a huge cuirass that is too big, and he can't see over it very well. He's holding this big heavy scroll. It is so long that he has trouble lifting it. Comedic proportions. He carries it out to the podium, sets it down, and starts his speech.

"He says, like they do, 'Never before have we seen such a multitude gathered from every part of the world as we see today at my funeral. Today, at the Grove of the Caesars, we celebrate all my achievements and remember together the harmony and glory of my reign while I was alive. As a favor to you and all the nations, I will recite all the brutal things that I did to establish the dominion of the empire and elicit gratitude from the subjugated peoples.' Like a Res Gestae, from the underside. Right then an actor dressed as a lamb walks out on all fours, in front of the podium, and interrupts the whole thing. The lamb just grazes around and ignores him, as if nothing is happening. The emperor is annoyed and tries to continue, but he loses his place on the scroll. He points to someone to come get the lamb, but no one comes.

"So he keeps reading. 'Using my imperial might, I invaded countless lands. In awe of my health and well-being, kings begged for my clemency, and I granted them the privilege of calling me Father. Following in the footsteps of the deified Julius Caesar, I liberated the Republic from its Republicity. Out of the purest generosity, I did not interrupt or decline the grain supply because I alone believed that people should eat. At enormous expense, I restored enormous palaces and accepted enormous honors (with protest, of course). I had 3500 wild beasts slaughtered. I gave a million sesterces to the man who said he saw me going up into heaven. In recognition of my achievements, I spread the gospel of myself, and I am honored by the title of Savior."

A woman sitting near Batos spoke up. "I thought this play would have games."

"He's going on too long," Batos said to her. "I think that's part of the point."

She was unfazed by his answer. "Will there be animals?"

"Yes," Batos said and returned to The Story. "The animals are the athletes in the games. The emperor is wrapping it up. He says, 'Let time begin. Let the games begin.' Walking out into the space in front of the podium, is a ram, a bull, a lion, a crab, a fox, a fish. Let me see. Who else was there?" Batos counted on his hand. "There was an archer, someone with a water jug, and a butcher balance scale lady."

The person sitting by Kaineus shouted "The costumes! And the fabric! That manager is a genius. I want to be the crab."

"I'll be the archer," Kaineus added, raising her hand.

"The first game is a wrestling match between the Bull and Ram," Batos said. "Except the match gets cancelled because the Lamb peed in the oil that the wrestlers put on beforehand."

Laughter stirred the group. Virgos suppressed a smile.

"All the games, one after another, get disrupted because the Lamb does something. He doesn't get to play, but he wanders around in the paths of runners and chews the poles for the jumpers so that the poles fall down. He does all kinds of things that make the crowd cheer."

"I would cheer," Virgos said.

"The second game was a footrace with the Crab, the Scorpion, and this two-headed person. Gemini, I think it was. The race starts, and the Crab pulls ahead. He's faster because he has lots of legs. The Scorpion has to slow down because he's carrying the weight of his own weapon. The two headed person can't make up their mind, so they run part of the way and then stop. The Lamb comes out and trips the Crab. The crab falls, and the Scorpion stops. No one wins.

"At this point, the emperor is angry. The Games established in his honor are falling apart. He has a trophy in front of him on the podium, and he doesn't get to present it to the winner. Oh, yeah, I forgot. There's an ass."

Two in the group seemed to agree on this as they raised their voices. "Yes, there is an ass. More than one."

Batos pointed at the two in the group who had spoken. "You speak the truth." He continued, "The ass is wearing a purple blanket. It has his name on it—Chamberlain—and he has been standing next to the emperor the entire time. He decides he has heard enough, and he turns around, and kicks the podium to the ground. It sends the trophy flying. The Lamb comes over to the trophy and stomps on it. Breaks it into pieces."

Myrina spoke softly. "This is going to take a turn."

"The emperor is furious," Batos continued. "He takes a sword and pierces the side of the Lamb. The Lamb dies right there, in the space where the stage should be."

"The Lamb of God," Myrina said.

Batos' voice grew louder as he remembered the character of the emperor. "'I am the Son of God,' the emperor says. The emperor takes the Lamb's leg, drags him to a ditch, and throws him onto a burning garbage dump. He picks up the trophy and tries to put it back together, but the pieces won't fit. Someone comes running into the crowd and says, 'The body is gone!'"

The group anticipated the next step of The Story and spoke over one another with excitement. "He is risen! He is risen from the dead!"

Batos savored the excitement in the room. "The emperor doesn't believe it. He sends his wife to the garbage dump to find out what happened. She comes back and says, 'The body is gone.' Then the Lamb appears on top of the arch," Batos voice softened. He paused. "The Lamb was bloody, but He was alive. He stood above all of them. The emperor, the broken trophy, the shredded ropes. The lion, who had been silent up to this point, speaks. 'There shall be no more death. All glory to the Lamb who has conquered death. He is the Savior of the world and all worlds to come. There is no place he has not been. No pit he has not seen.'

Batos grew silent and allowed the group to add their own meaning. Three members proclaimed what they heard.

"The Lamb has risen."

"The Passover Lamb."

"Jesus is the Lamb. Thank you, Lord Jesus."

"The lion turns to the audience." Batos said. "She turns to me. She says, 'I leave you with the peace of the Lord Jesus. Amen and amen.'"

Batos found himself standing in the center of the room, looking up at the ceiling, with one arm raised. The room spun, and he felt dizzy. He did not know where he was. The group was silent. Some held back tears. Others bowed their heads. His eyes followed the couches around the room and then to the open door. He was aware of the eyes of the group, but also the eyes of a small creature. It was a marten. The marten stared at him with a penetrating gaze. Had the marten been there all along? As the group exploded in applause, the marten curled himself and vanished.

Chapter 23

Kaineus

KAINEUS AWOKE WITHOUT THE usual headache of a wine-filled evening. She had slept in longer than expected. Virgos and Batos were nowhere in sight, and the room was empty. She untied her hair and tied it again so that the loose strands stayed in place. Stepping out into the room with the couches, she saw Leah in her chair, poring over a papyrus scroll. Lists of numbers and words lined up across it.

Leah looked up and smiled at Kaineus. "Welcome," she said, setting down the scroll on a side table. "These ledgers never end, but I do enjoy working with numbers. And I like money," she said without apology. "It allows us to do what we do." She gestured toward a table of food and drink. "May I offer anything? Pomegranate juice? I have some lovely dates, and I have the most delicious figs. Bread with honey perhaps? Sometimes I step outside of myself and put all of them together!" Kaineus was intrigued by this woman and her ease of leadership. This morning she was wearing a turban and caftan that was painted with rose petals. A ruby glowed at her forehead.

"What is it that you do?" Kaineus asked, her mouth full of fig.

"Most people don't know what we do. First and foremost, we are a creative house. We are a group of playwrights, actors, builders, and technicians. The rich citizens here in Adramyttium and elsewhere hire us to write new work, often for their dinner parties. They want short plays, comedies, and light entertainment that does not challenge them in any way. They pay us well for it. I enjoy feeding them the fantasies and literary delicacies they like to eat. You know the stories they like: plebians who need guidance and protection, the glory of the gods, whatever preserves their entitlement. Our group also does custom funeral rites for those who want a more elaborate ceremony or for those who desire discretion."

Kaineus could imagine the group performing these plays after dinner, but she had seen more than that the night before. She had seen a depth of belief and a tinge of rebellion. "Do you write plays about Jesus of Nazareth?" she asked.

"One of my playwrights is working on one now. As far as the public is concerned, it's a delicate balance of creativity and survival. The wisdom of Jesus puzzles the world. Storytellers like Batos bring us new inspiration." Leah did not explain further. She reached for her own cup and sat next to Kaineus on the couch.

Kaineus thought on the possibility of a custom funeral rite. "You should have been at my husband's funeral," she said.

"Was it dull?" Leah asked.

Kaineus laughed with relief of being understood. "Only my friend Virgos made it bearable. An oil merchant asked my mother about my next marriage. He wanted to be a candidate. That would have been worse than before. I would not consider it. I ran." Leah made a small affirming sound. "Looking at it now, marriage was a space I occupied. It was the same for my husband. A pragmatic arrangement."

"What spaces appeal to you now?" Leah asked.

"Only those I can design and determine for myself," Kaineus said. "But there are people who will see that as impossible."

"No town is free of petty tyrants. But their worlds are small."

Kaineus was curious about this woman's story. "How long have you led this house?"

"My husband and I led it until his death a few years ago. Now it is mine," Leah said. "He was a giant of a man. A virile Macedonian. The wasting disease took him. His body ate itself, and all of his strength could not overcome it. In his last days, he dreamed many plays. I wrote them down and stored them in jars in the basement. They are seeds waiting to grow." She pointed to the couch on the opposite side of the room. "He laid on that couch over there for several days after his death. I could hear his spirit say, 'I'm starting to turn color, Fern.' That was his nickname for me. 'Go find yourself another Bacchus,' he said." She smiled at the memory and took a deep breath.

"Was he a . . . believer . . . ?" Kaineus did not know the right word to use.

"Oh yes," Leah said. "Publicly, we nod in all the right directions. In our house, Jesus is Lord. I rather like the multilingual nature of it. Providing the elite with the praise they crave, and at the same time, using their funds to write plays to subvert them. It involves strategy, this business, straddling the two worlds. And you?" Leah asked calmly and directly. "What do you believe?"

Kaineus had no clear answer. "Something happened to me during that play in Pergamum, and again here last night. The freedom of these people, the ways they imagine and move together. They are free in every way. And it seems to come from deep within them. They do what their convictions calls them to do. There is no interference or hesitation. Does the message of Jesus of Nazareth help them do that? Did Paul of Tarsus help them do that?" Kaineus paused, and Leah remained silent. "What I like most is that it is real to them. It's not just something you do outwardly because someone tells you to do it. I want something real."

"What we have here is real, but we are only symbols and signs. We point to a much larger message and meaning. The good news is not ours. For that, you must keep travelling."

Virgos and Batos walked into the room, talking animatedly about spices. Leah touched Kaineus' shoulder kindly in recognition of what they had shared. Batos said, "The time has come," he said. They walked together down the stairs and out the front door, where the horses were saddled and waiting.

Myrina had just returned from the agora with a full jar of ointment. She handed it to Virgos, and he thanked her. "It will itch and flake," she said. "Allow it to do both. The body has its own wisdom."

Projecting her voice to the group, Leah said, "You are all welcome here, at any time, for any reason." They climbed up into their saddles, and the horses started moving of their own accord. "Tell Paul that he is welcome here too. I would like to meet him someday."

Chapter 24

Virgos

THE PREDICTION OF ITCH had come true. Virgos forced himself not to pick at the wounds on his head and face. "The body has its own wisdom," Myrina had said. He was curious about that phrase. As far as he knew, he had the only copy of Wisdom outside of Alexandria. Were there others? Where would the wisdom of the body be written? If he had the opportunity, he would return to Adramyttium to talk with her.

They had set off in the opposite direction, however. Sitting in his saddle, he turned around to look behind him. They were waiting for Kaineus. She had fallen behind on the path. The horse stood still and would not move until they caught up. "Thank you for waiting," she said to him as she approached. "I had trouble getting back on." He could imagine her being frustrated about the inconvenience, but her smile was quick and relaxed.

"We will go into the Promised Land together. Even though it is the wrong one," Virgos said.

"Going to Thessalonica will be worth it. You'll see. I just know it. Paul is going to answer questions you didn't know you had."

"I am fully aware of all of my questions," Virgos admonished her. She was unfazed.

"How far are we going today?" she asked.

"Assos. I am eager to see it. Aristotle started an academy there and tutored Alexander of Macedon. I will pray for the blessings of the ancestors."

"I have heard of the sarcophagi there," Kaineus said. "A unique local stone. And I remember my mother commenting on their relationship with Emperor Gaius. Of course, that history would be subdued now."

Batos met them on the trail and stood in front, facing them. He had been checking the route ahead. "The path is clear. I don't anticipate any problems from here to Assos. Adequate water. If all goes well, we should be there by dark." The horses stood with their heads together. They made a triangle of companions. Batos untied a small bag of dried fruit that Leah had given them for the trip. He offered it to Kaineus, who took a handful and passed it to Virgos. They had grown comfortable with one another.

"How's the head?" Batos asked Virgos.

"I was gifted from my youth." Virgos quoted the Wisdom scroll.

Batos nodded. "I do not doubt it. How are your wounds?"

"I used the rose oil and resin this morning, and it has eased the itch somewhat. The dry land shall be glad, and the desert shall rejoice and blossom," Virgos responded with thoughts of Isaiah. He was not certain that they always understood his allusions, but he enjoyed making them anyway. The images of blooms in the desert soothed him.

Batos looked down at the mare's mane, but he was lost in thought. "The desert bloom is a beautiful thing," he said.

Taking in the view to their left, they saw a glimmer of water on the horizon. The trail they followed had turned to follow the coast but stayed north of the main road. Batos had insisted on staying off the main road for their safety. On the side of the trail, Virgos noticed a pattern of stones lying next to one another. The stones looked as if they had been arranged intentionally. He glanced at Kaineus, who seemed to be looking at it as well. She cocked her head to one side and made an inquisitive sound.

Virgos swung his leg over the saddle and jumped down to the ground. He knelt in front of the stones. "Is this a letter?" he asked. Kaineus did the same, followed by Batos.

"There's more than one letter," she said, kneeling next to him. She traced the first line of stones, and pointed to a second. "And look at these," she said, tracing additional letters with her finger.

Batos stood as the other two knelt. "It says 'Justice.'"

Virgos was fascinated. "In what language?"

"Lyconian."

"Who would spell out Justice with stones? And why?" Kaineus asked.

"This is probably a gravesite. See where the ground rises up there, and the larger stone above?" He pointed to a swell and then a heavy piece of granite at the top. "Someone was buried here," Batos said.

"A poor man's inscription," Virgos said.

"A poor man's prayer," said Kaineus.

"A prayer, or a warning," Batos said.

Virgos and Kaineus stood and they studied the letters together. Virgos turned to Batos and asked, "How do you know Lyconian?"

"I know several languages. I travelled around and picked up words and conversations here and there. My mother was a Celt. She taught me 'the old language,' as she called it, and that was my first. She wouldn't speak anything else." He swung himself up into the saddle. Virgos wondered if Batos enjoyed being cryptic. There was much to learn from him.

"Let's go. Leave this person in peace," Batos said.

Kaineus was thoughtful as they resumed the usual pace of travel. "Have you ever thought of what you would like on your funeral monument?" she asked Virgos.

He had thought more of where his tomb would be rather than what would be written on it. "I want it to be in Jerusalem," he said. "God will give me a monument. A future and a name. I will let God decide what to say." He turned to Kaineus. "What would you like on your monument?"

"Just my name," she said.

Virgos was interested to hear what Batos might say to this. "What do you think, Batos? What would you like?"

"I want to be buried in the earth. Somewhere near the water. That's what our bodies are. Earth and water. But like you, I know that's out of my hands," he said.

Without being asked, the horses started to trot of their own accord. They had pricked up their ears and rumbled low nickers to each other. They were of one mind. "What is happening?" Virgos asked.

"They know where we are," Batos said. "We're almost to Assos. They have a friend here."

Chapter 25

Batos

in his own words

LET ME CATCH YOU up. It's dark. The moon is almost full. I've been watching the animal traders outside of the city. I've got my route planned. Which cages to open first, which latches will slide silently, how to get in and out. Remember? That's not how it turned out. But I'll get there.

I decide to start with the leopards. I trot up to the first cage, soft-footed and bent low. The cage is big, on wheels, with two leopards inside. They of course saw me from far off and watched my approach. They pace and switch back and forth in front of each other. Their mouths are open, and I can see their teeth. The latch on the cage door opens fairly easily, and the door swings wide. I duck back around behind the cage so they would have a clear exit and wouldn't see me on the way out. Thinking about it now, I don't know who I was fooling. They knew exactly where I was and could have torn me apart just for spite. But they gave me a reprieve, jumped out one after the other, and disappeared. I always liked cats.

On to the ostriches. Two surprisingly tall birds, taller than me. They turn to me at the gate of their small pen. Each one has one foot forward, and that front toe looks like it could slice me open. Same approach for me here: open, duck out of the way. They don't fly, but they might as well have. Sprinters couldn't have kept up.

The flamingoes were next. They had gathered in a group at the far back corner of the pen. You can't tell a flamingo to do anything. You just have to wait.

I stopped to cut circle nets and hand nets and snares. My knife slices easily through the rope. I bend the snares so that the wire weakens and won't hold. If you bend it back the other direction, sometimes you can break the back of a snare. Then it's not a snare anymore. Just a piece of wire you can use for something else. One pen had been broken into pieces already. The fences were laid flat and splintered. That must have been where the elephant was.

As I'm cutting nets, the flamingoes decide that an open gate is a good thing, and that it could lead them somewhere. They squawk and honk at each other. They don't fly, even though they could have lifted themselves off the ground. They run together as a group into the dark. Eventually they will take flight, and no one will be able to capture them in the air.

So, as far as the animals, three cages down, two to go. The card players are still lost in their game. I need them to focus on the game, to keep their heads down, so they wouldn't see the giraffe. How could they not see a giraffe? I haven't had much to do with giraffes, up close anyway, but I have heard stories about their hooves. 'Avoid the stomp' was the order I received. Understood. I was given that order from someone who didn't, so there's an eyewitness.

The giraffe is standing up. When it was lying down, I had trouble figuring out what it was. But now there is no question. The giraffe has been watching the leopards, ostriches, flamingoes, and me. I can't tell the look on her face because of the low light. I can't tell if she's mad or just watching. Whatever it is, I have to keep moving, so I slip the rope latch over the top of the pole, and step off to the side. I wait for whatever comes next. She walks slowly up to me—those hooves are magnificent—and she looks down at me over the gate. She looks directly at me. She isn't mad. Those big dark eyes. Kindness, I guess it was. Kindness in a place filled with cruelty. I get choked up when I think about it. A quiet gentleness shown by one creature to another. She steps out of the pen and then launches herself forward with power, like a fast horse.

The plan is going well up to this point. They're all out and on their way. Now the loudest ones were left. Here we go.

The pigs are only one step away from true wild, captured in the early stages of fences. They are hairy, muscular, and mean. I don't blame them for the mean. They didn't have a choice about the other two things. One pen, about thirty of them, mostly sows. As I watch, one sow moves to the side and I see little piglets. A recent litter. I can't repeat what I said then. Sows with babies are ferocious. And they scream when they're angry.

The same approach with latches and gates applies in theory, but this time with a complication. The rope used to tie the gate to the pole was tied under the top rung, so I wouldn't be able to slip it over the top. And perched on the flat surface of the opposite fence pole is a statue of Tiberius. It is a marble bust that has clearly been there for a while. Someone had tied the corners of its base to the top of the fence pole so it would stay there, but the rope was loose. One smarty had made a sign around the emperor's neck. It said 'Biberius.'" Apparently he was a drinker. The bust being perched there means that I would have to cut the rope without bumping into anything and knocking it off the fence pole. If it fell, the statue would make noise, break, and get everyone excited.

I approach and kneel in front of the rope latch. It was thick. I start sawing and get about halfway through when I bumped the other side of the gate with my elbow. The statue wobbles but stays put. I start sawing again, but the pigs are restless. Milling around, probably planning their exit just like I am. I am almost through the rope, I make one cut from the opposite side, and it splits. I say "Yes!" Two pieces of rope, one in each hand.

This is what I was saying in the beginning. It didn't go to plan.

When the rope splits, I bump the fence pole again with my elbow. The statue of Tiberius falls backwards into the pen. It breaks, cracks, makes this hollow sound. One of the sows screams, and the rest of them join in. It's like a choir. The animal traders look up from their game, stand up, and start running toward us. By 'us,' I mean me and thirty sows and about ten babies. I am right where I should not be, between forty angry hogs and the open country. I'm on all fours and start crawling as fast as I can to get out of the way. I feel the first bite on the back of my calf—still got a hole there—and then their hooves on my back and the back of my head. It's harder to crawl when you're being stampeded.

Eventually the herd is on its way. The trampling stops. By then I am out of the pen, but only a few steps ahead of the traders. I have to turn on the speed to get out of there. They give up the chase as we get farther and farther away from the settlement. I could hear the last one breathing behind me and then stop. I think I heard him fall, but it doesn't matter if he did or not. The leopards probably got him either way.

Chapter 26

Kaineus

THE WAVES OF THE sea reflected the late summer sun. At least she thought the glimpse of blue between green clumps of pine was the sea. She had imagined greeting the sea with a calm, peaceful gaze, but instead, she was bouncing up and down on top of a horse. This gray mare was on a mission, and she had to hold on. The sea would have to wait.

Entering the gates of Assos, she recognized the architecture of a city eager for imperial attention. The pace had slowed to a determined walk with Batos in the lead. They walked through the center of a large necropolis and reached the agora. "We're going to the stable," he called back to her and Virgos. Rounding a corner behind the line of shops, Batos said, "Ifran!"

A man with close-cropped black hair turned toward him, and a wide smile spread across his face. He raised one hand and said, "My friends have come to visit! And you brought Batos with you!"

Kaineus had never met this man, but she could not help but smile at the affectionate teasing. She felt herself staring at him. His skin was like liquid bronze poured over onyx. He was taller than Batos, but not by much, and the two looked like brothers. She could not discern if they were related by blood or by friendship. Batos swung his leg over and hopped to the ground. The chestnut mare stepped forward to Ifran and bumped him in the chest with the flat of her forehead. "Still butting people with your head, I see," said the man.

"She missed you," Batos said.

The two of them embraced and began talking in a language that was unlike any she had ever heard. She took in the waterfall of sound and forced herself to look away. Virgos was intrigued but had no compulsion to look away. Returning to Greek, Batos introduced them to one another. "Ifran will take care of the horses while we look around and get something to eat," he said.

"Where is the theater?" Kaineus asked.

"Close to the water," Batos said. "We can go check it out. It will be dark soon, and today's shows will be over." Kaineus noticed that Batos was staring at something in the distance. He had stopped moving and grown quiet. She tried to look where he was looking, to see what he saw, but she saw only the temple of Athena. Images of Herakles, centaurs, and other animals were carved in the tympanum and architraves. But why would a temple keep his attention? "Is everything alright?" Kaineus asked.

"That's not what lions look like," he muttered. "The theater is this way."

Smaller in scale than the massive theater at Pergamum, the theater at Assos seemed to hang off the edge of the cliff overlooking the sea. The three of them stood at the top, looking out over the seats, the stage area, and the sea beyond. Kaineus' mind started to imagine a production there. "Let's make up a play," she said. Instantly, the other two agreed, and they started down the center aisle.

"I want to sit in the senator's seat," she said as she entered the first row of seats.

Batos was close behind her. "I'll sit in the actor's seat," he said. "They sit in the same row, right?" he said, nudging her elbow with his.

Virgos took center stage and opened his arms like a host. The last of the sunlight disappeared behind the horizon, and silver threads of cloud hung in its wake. The cool wind carried a touch of autumn. "Welcome to all! We have a new show planned for tonight, the first of its kind. Tonight you will see an improvisational apocalypse. All the stars are here tonight: the Javelins, the Long Hairs, and the Blood Red Comets. We welcome Persephone and the orchestra down in the pit," Virgos gestured to the stone floor of the stage. "The horn section looks particularly strong. We welcome the Emperor who is in attendance." He pointed to the top row of seats. "We probably look small to you down here on the stage, but we often do. We have a bit of bad news for you tonight. None of our gladiators are available. They are all in weaving class, and so our show will not include gladiators. We apologize and will do our best in their absence."

Kaineus stepped out of the first row and walked hurriedly up to Virgos. She whispered in his ear. Virgos continued, "It seems that we have run out of blood. Previous apocalypses have drained the trough of blood. Tonight's destruction will be bloodless. But we here at the Assos theater strive to provide our audiences with the savagery that you desire. Kaineus, we begin the show with you."

Turning toward the seats, she raised her arms and said one word. "Exordium!" Moving to the side, she awaited the next development from Virgos.

"We open the curtain to a time of Zechariah. Imagine a stage set with myrtle trees and golden lampstands. The word of the Lord came to a man named Branch. Standing at his side was a priest, and they had a peaceful understanding." Stepping to his side, Kaineus stood by Virgos as the priest. "The people of the Lord have refused to listen. They have ignored the words of the prophets and gone their own way. The Lord of hosts will render judgment against them for their sins: prejudice, domination, envy, exploiting the widow and the orphan, brutality toward all living creatures, and praying to a thing that is dead." Virgos turned to Kaineus and said, "Is that a good list? Is there anything you would like to add?" Kaineus shook her head and gestured for him to continue. "Like mice in a pot, they have devoured one another, feeding off the weak and silencing the mirth of the small ones. Because they have ignored the prophets and broken the commandments, they will now be destroyed.

"An earthquake will shake the foundations of the cities and cause great chasms to open between the mountains. Mount Ida will vomit and spew fire." Kaineus added sound effects and made the shape of a volcano eruption with her arms. "There will be a plague of gnats." She swiped the air as if surrounded by a swarm. "There will be plagues of frogs and flies. There will be armies of locusts and ghosts of ancient war horses. A flying sickle will dismember the rulers of the earth. Hooks will drag the pieces of their bodies in the streets and cast them into the river. The river will swallow them and spit out the hook. There will be thirst and the absence of quail. The people will suffer greatly. They will call out to the Lord for forgiveness." Kaineus, who had been acting out each of these scenes, suppressed her laughter. Virgos smiled mischievously at her, and seemed to have more punishment in store.

Batos stood suddenly and walked to the center of the aisle. His face was somber. He spread his arms wide and straight out from his shoulders. "I intercede for them."

Kaineus and Virgos were stunned. Why did he stretch out his arms?

Batos repeated his words, "I intercede for them. I will suffer on a cross in their stead."

Virgos asked him, "Are you the prophet who has come to show us the way?"

"Yes," said Batos.

"Are you aware that this path will cost you your life?" asked Virgos.

"Yes," he responded.

"Are you willing to take their sins upon yourself?"

"I am," Batos said.

Batos walked to center stage and faced the seats. He spread out his arms again and let his head fall. Kaineus and Virgos stood silent. He was playing the role of Jesus of Nazareth. He did not move. He merely stood with his head hanging low.

Kaineus stepped toward Batos and stood behind him. She folded one arm in toward his chest, and then the other arm. He fell backwards into her. She caught him as his head fell back onto her shoulder. She lowered his body to the stage and laid him on his back.

With Kaineus back at his side, Virgos said, "Wisdom has dwelt with us and descended into Sheol. We pray for the resurrection, when we will be reunited, when we are caught up together in spirit." Virgos improvised a graveside address.

"Step out of your earthly tent.
Out of the walls that hide the light.
Let the hooded cape fall
Lift your eyes and feast on stars
The hope that was within you
Now a summons unmuffled
Where I AM you will be also
Grafted together
Climbing stone and crevasse
Root and tendril combined
Until the temple glows with green
And all the earth grows as one."

Kaineus began a verse of her own.

"Draw your son to you
Unfurl the wings of your horses
Rise to you on golden wing
Receive your son, a man of your own making
His deeds inscribed on our hearts
Virtues emblazoned on those near him
A monument of memory for all time."

She glanced at Virgos to indicate that she had finished. Batos, who had been listening, began to stand. On his feet, he turned to them with a smile.

Virgos spoke, "As the prophet Isaiah has foretold, your dead shall live. Their corpses shall rise. Those who dwell in the dust, awake and sing for joy. Your dew is radiant, and the earth will give birth to those long dead. He has returned from death. The gate of Wisdom is open."

Kaineus felt moisture on her face. It was tears, but a light rain had also begun to fall. A rumble of thunder echoed across the water. Virgos turned his head toward the sound of thunder and said, "And God says, 'Amen!'"

Chapter 27

Batos

THE SMELL OF WET clay rose from the floor of the cave. He was standing, but his feet were mired in clay up to the ankles. He was unable to lift his feet or take a step in any direction. Clay had dried on his clothes and his hands. The cave walls were made of gleaming yellow marble and veined with red coral. A lampstand stood in each corner of the room, and lamps lined the base of each wall. His eyes tried to adjust to the low light.

Off to his left, he saw movement. He looked and he saw a man standing. The man was wearing striped breeches and had the appearance of a Parthian warrior. His hair was parted in the middle and braided in the back. His beard was tied into a single braid at his chin. He was writing on the wall of the cave with a stylus. Three Hebrew letters were complete: *yod, hey, vav*. As he began to write the fourth letter, he turned to face Batos. He placed a vertical index finger over his mouth and made a gesture for silence. Then he turned his back again and continued to write.

Batos turned his face toward the center of the cave floor. Something shifted position in the dark. He saw bones. Some reflected the light. Others lay in shadow. They began to move toward one another and search for one another. As if pulled by a great wind, the bones rolled and lifted themselves. Those who claimed to conquer did not acknowledge the bones that were knitting themselves together deep in the earth. They rattled and danced toward each other with notes only other bones can hear. Their song of percussion grew until it became a deafening roar. End to end, the bones formed sinews and sewed themselves together into the frame of a human. The human did not kneel. She stood.

After the bones were formed, skin and muscles grew over the frame. Dressed in a striped tunic and breeches, a Parthian woman warrior stood before him. Hair stretched down her back. A bow was at her feet, and in her hand was a cup made of clay. A cross was smeared on the cup with red dust. From the cup arose the smell of vinegar. She extended the cup to him.

The man writing on the wall had completed a fourth letter. It was a Hebrew letter *hey*, forming the holy name of the Lord. The lamps on the floor grew into pillars. Smoke from them filled the room so that he could no longer see fire. He could hear the crackle of flames and wind above. Then he heard a voice calling out to Rome:

> "I resist
> I resist
> I resist
> Mortal, can these bones live? O Lord God, you know.
> Dancing out of their graves
> They call to one another
> I am here and have always been here
> Now is our dance
> Now is the cue
> Draw together
> Commune
> Draw together until the scattered and broken can bear
> weight and stand upright
> I look up to you no longer."

Chapter 28

Batos

BATOS DRIFTED IN THE space between awake and asleep. He was lying on his back on the stage at Assos with his cloak rolled under his head. His eyes were closed. The images were flooding in fast. They flowed into one another and then back again. He had been in a cave of fire. Then, in the way of dreams, he was lying on the forest floor with a woman he knew and loved. The face of Raven was above him. He saw rain on her brown skin and felt strands of her wet hair on his neck. He followed the path of a single rain-drop on the curve of her hip and felt rain streaming down her naked back into his hand.

"You are not here," he said into the empty space above him. He made a guttural sound and stood. He stood up too quickly and felt a wave of dizziness. He looked at his friends. Kaineus was asleep in the niche of the footspace between stone seats. She had tucked herself in under the ledge of the seat above. Her arms were flung above her head. Virgos was asleep in much the same way in another section of seats, but one arm was curled around his scroll case. He held it close to his body.

Batos had not been down to the harbor yet, so he set off in the violet light of morning to find the trail down to the water. It was a long and steep descent. His foot slipped on small stones,

and he caught himself with the other heel. Lightning shot out of
the ends of his fingers, and one knee creaked with the sudden
responsibility. Annoyed, he shook his head. When he reached the
water, he felt his shoulders relax. He sat cross legged in the rocky
shore mud and started to untie the leather straps of his boots. Setting his boots neatly to the side, he unwound the cloth of his foot
bindings and set those near his boots. When he stood on his bare
feet, he felt the stones give way into the soft soil beneath him. He
winced at the feel of rocks on the bottoms of his feet. His desert
calluses had long since softened.

The glass surface of the water was warm, but it was cool and
refreshing underneath. He waded in until the water reached his
ankles. Reaching down for a handful of water, he raised the little
cup to his face and rinsed the dust off his forehead. He looked out
at the horizon line of the island across the water. It reminded him
of another horizon: a mountain ridge and a siege in the name of
Tacfarinas. Tacfarinas had been killed by the Romans, but he had
inspired a rebellion that would not die. Surrounded by his brothers
and sisters of the Musulamii, Batos shouted the name of their rebel
leader and summoned their courage for the siege ahead. Raw with
grief, he stood with his chosen tribe, side by side on horseback,
before they charged forward against the Roman invaders.

Batos came back to the moment and the ring of water around
his ankles. He heard the slide of boot on pebbles behind him. He
held his head very still as he looked down and to the right. The
water was below him, but he could not see water. Out of his chest,
smeared with a faint sheen, was the angled corner of an arrow-
head. The arrow had travelled through his back and ribs. He heard
another movement and reached for his knife at his waist with his
left hand. Step to the right. Transfer weight to the ball of your foot.
Spin. Raise your arm and elbow. Throw.

Spinning rhythmically, the knife cut through the air and
lodged with a gulping sound into the throat of the man. The impact
of the knife threw him back into the scrub. The branches parted,
and he fell hard onto his back. He gurgled and choked on the knife.
A bow fell from his hand.

Batos saw the knife hit the target and heard the gulping sound. His face was wet. He had fallen forward, face down into the water. Waters enveloped him now, sky and earth and water together. He heard all of creation beckoning him back to where he was made. You are one of us. You are precious. Voices of birds and fish. Worms and all creeping things. Come back. Return to us. You are home.

Chapter 29

Virgos

"YOU MAKE A GOOD volcano," Virgos said to Kaineus as they descended the trail to the harbor. "It was very realistic."

Kaineus laughed. "I heard that you could make the sound of thunder by rolling stones around inside a copper bowl. Wouldn't that make a great sound? I wonder how Leah's people do sound for their plays."

Virgos looked up at the violet skies. "We might not need to make the sound of thunder. God might do the sound today." Weaving through shrubs and short trees bent by weather, the path was dry but carved into the steep incline of the cliff. "Does anyone build a city on a flat plain? Why all this climbing?"

"Hilltops are easier to defend," she said.

"Moses must have been an athlete. How many times did he go up and down the mountain to talk to God?"

"I don't know those stories," Kaineus said. She reached out for a woody branch to steady her descent.

"I hope Paul can teach us both," Virgos said. He was aware that he had not voiced this hope before. Perhaps it had been there all along, but he had not put it into words.

They stepped around a shrub and saw a man lying face up on the shore. Both stopped abruptly. "Who is that?" Kaineus asked. A knife was lodged in his throat. Fear gripped her as she held Virgos' gaze.

"He was at the stream when I was attacked. He stood and watched," Virgos said.

"That is Batos' knife. Where is he?" She looked around in a frenzy and saw the end of an arrow emerging from the surface of the water. Virgos followed close behind her as she cried out and splashed toward his body. Batos was lying face down. They reached under his arms and lifted him up. Struggling to find footing, slipping on pebbles, they pulled him toward the shore. Virgos pitched forward with the weight and went under. He found the shoulder of Batos again and kept pulling. When they reached the water's edge, they fell back, one on either side of Batos. Kaineus was breathing hard with panic. Virgos felt a deep sadness well up within him. The sadness was quiet and still, like the silence of a well.

"This can't be! This can't be!" shouted Kaineus as she sat up. Reaching around behind his back, she grasped the arrow with both hands and snapped it in half. They rolled Batos onto his back and eased out the front half of the arrow from his chest. Water and blood oozed from the wound. His eyes were closed, and his face had a peaceful expression. She closed her eyes and let out a sharp, angry roar. "What can we do? Can you say something that will bring him back? Can you pray him back? Isn't that what your God does?" she pleaded.

"He's gone," Virgos said quietly. "He has been taken up." He was beyond their reach now.

"But how can he be finished? And the man used a bow?!" she covered her face with her hand. "We asked him to take us to Thessalonica. What have we done?" She looked at Virgos with anguish and then turned on him. "Why are you so calm? Don't you see what has happened here?"

"He knew the risks," Virgos said. "Prophets know the risks. They do it anyway."

Kaineus seemed to collapse into herself. She placed both hands on the top of her head. "Stay in it," she said softly to herself. "Do not run. Stay here."

Virgos sat in silence for a moment. He reached over Batos' body and touched her elbow. "We need to move him." She did not seem to understand. "We need to bury him."

Kaineus shook her head with frustration. "You are moving too fast! What is wrong with you?" she shouted. She looked around at the stony shore. "There is no soil here. Only rocks. We have nothing to dig with. Should we find Ifran?" Both looked up at the steep ascent that led them down to the harbor. "Can we carry him up the hill?" she asked.

"We cannot leave him here," Virgos said firmly.

Kaineus looked nauseous. She swallowed and met his eyes. "We cannot leave him here," she repeated.

She stood, and Virgos followed. He said, "I will lift him by his feet, and you can lift him by his arms."

Kaineus looked toward his boots and bindings sitting neatly together by the water. "His boots," she said in a short staccato burst.

Virgos picked them up and brought them to the feet of Batos. Batos had not been wearing shoes the day that they met him. A barefoot Moses who led his people through the wilderness. "Help me put them on," he said. Kaineus knelt down near him. They wound the bindings around his bare feet. They slid on his boots, one at a time, and tied the laces at the top. Suddenly she stood and walked angrily toward the body of man who killed him. "Do not do it," Virgos warned. "It will not ease your grief."

But she did not seem to hear him. She yanked Batos' knife out of his throat. Gripping the knife, she crouched over his body. It was as if she was deciding what to do.

"Kaineus, it will not bring Batos back," Virgos said firmly.

She breathed deeply and squared her shoulders. She looked at the man from the bottom to the top and said, "Let the wolves eat him."

Chapter 30

Kaineus

"WE CANNOT LEAVE HIM here," she heard Virgos say. She knew that to be true and fixed. The knife in her hand and the steep trail did not change either. But nothing, not even Virgos' strange calm, would cause her to move until she chose to move.

She stepped over to Batos and sat beside him. She did not want to be where she was, but she did not want to leave. Feeling the small stones give way beneath her, she laid down beside Batos on her back. It was as if they were childhood friends, seeing shapes in the clouds. The shoulder of his tunic was wet against her shoulder. She breathed in the sounds and the smells of the moment that she would never have again. She heard the subtle shift of Virgos' position nearby and a note of bird song. Peaceful sounds that did not fit the turmoil within her.

She closed her eyes and allowed herself to drift into a memory. The memory took her to Ephesus, when her father was chosen as Asiarch. It was not yet sunset in Ephesus, and the late afternoon sun brought sweat to her forehead. Sitting with her mother in the crowded stadium, she smelled bodies and heard layers of languages, but the eyes of the crowd studied them as if they did not belong. Such attention was typical for the family of a public figure, but their gaze held more than curiosity. In the swirl of senses, she felt menace.

The mechanical gate of the stadium entrance rolled up slowly with a series of sharp clicks. Standing in a chariot behind two giant horses, her father entered the stadium with a parade smile. Jeers rose from the crowd, and the noise of shouting surrounded them.

"Go back to Pergamum, Puppet!"

"Impotent! He is impotent!"

Claudia spoke into her daughter's ear in muted tones. "They say he is a Roman puppet, with no ability to reason on his own, but I suspect the problem is something else."

"What is that?" she asked.

"He is not Ephesian," Claudia said firmly.

Startled by the eruption of noise, the horses surged forward. They jerked the chariot forward in short bursts. The charioteer struggled to slow them. Her father steadied himself against the wall of the chariot. The chants and exclamations exploded and filled the stadium with a chaos of laughter and anger. Someone to her right stood and threw a stone at the horses, and it bounced off the hip of nearest one. The mare squealed in fury and threw her head. She bolted and dragged the other mare that was yoked to her.

More stones followed and struck the horses. Jumping and snorting, the horses were at odds with one another. One was furious and ready to charge forward, and the other locked her knees and planted her feet in the dust. The wooden beam that held the horses to the chariot could not handle the strain. The wood tore from the metal. No longer held upright by the beam, the chariot pitched forward. Her father and the charioteer tumbled over the front and fell into a pile of tangled limbs. Freed of their burden, the horses launched forward, leaning and pulling in opposite directions. They careened around the stadium and narrowly avoided a statue of Artemis. As they swerved around it, the statue fell face down and bounced as it was struck by the dragging hitch.

The crowd had become a senseless jumble of shrieks and stones flying through the air. Her mother fought to restrain her panic and whispered her husband's name, but Kaineus felt the confusion and anger of the horses. Furious and frightened beyond reason, they ran in endless circles. They ran past the door that would lead them to freedom. Around and around the track they ran, suffering the violence of the yoke and the crowd. Too bewildered to think and pulling against one another, they were trapped in the stadium and could not see their way out. There was no one to direct them to safety. There was no one to guide them.

"We need to leave before we become the target," Claudia said, dragging her up the stone stairs and out of the stadium.

"What about the horses?" Claudia did not respond. "What about the horses? Who will calm them? Who will guide them?"

Kaineus drifted out of the memory and back to the shoulder that touched hers. The warmth of his body was fading. The fabric of her own tunic was damp, and the stones of the water's edge jutted into her shoulder blades. She opened her eyes. Virgos was sitting where he had been, very still, with his hands folded. Batos was next to her, but he was gone.

The memory of the riot in Ephesus revealed its aim to her. These were the horses of her soul: frightened, passionate, furious. They were at odds with one another. They ran in circles with no one to guide them. She reached out to her mind with both hands as if she were reaching for a loved one. "I need you," she said aloud. She asked for the guidance of reason and wisdom. She asked for the ability to trust herself and her companions. "Show me the way."

She turned to Virgos. He was looking calmly at her. The fact that she had spoken aloud did not disturb his peace. "What is our next step?" he asked.

She slowly stood to her full height. "Our next step is uphill."

Chapter 31

Virgos

TOGETHER, THEY LIFTED THE body of Batos and began the climb. Walking backwards, Kaineus held his wrists in her hands. His body was wet and his limbs slipped. His head fell back and knocked against a stone with a sickening crunch. They lifted again and walked a few steps. One of his feet fell and dragged until Virgos could pick it up again. The awful horror of it made him sick.

Kaineus stopped and gently laid Batos down. "I will not do this. There has to be a better way," she said in a low voice.

"Put him on my back," Virgos said, and she nodded. He knelt near Batos. She lifted his torso from behind and wrapped his arms around Virgos' shoulders. Slowly Virgos stood and started walking up the hill. The mantle of Batos' body was light and easy to bear, but Virgos felt as if his gut were full of stones. The strange calm had faded to loss. As he climbed, he thought of the people who tended bodies and those who treated the dead with dignity. Did not the people carry Jacob? What of the others who did not have anyone to carry them? Was anyone with Jesus when he was crucified? Did anyone speak for the beaten and torn body of Jesus? He may never meet those people, but they were kin to him.

He heard Kaineus talking behind him. "This will end. This will not last forever. Sisyphus was a fool. Keep moving." She was speaking to herself, he was certain, as a form of encouragement. "The disregard for human life . . . why can't people show respect for life?" she asked.

Without stopping, Virgos said, "May I point out the irony of your assessment?"

"What are you talking about?" she said angrily.

"You skewered a man with an arrow and left another for the wolves."

She responded without hesitation. "And the two men you poisoned? They are probably still lying right where they were."

Virgos paused. He remembered handing bowls of food and hellebore to them with a genuine hope that they would suffer.

"All I'm saying is that Batos was different than them," she said. "He didn't deserve this," she said.

"Selah," Virgos said. The two fell into silence.

As they crested the hill, she said, "The necropolis is this way." He followed her to a group of sarcophagi near the east gate of the city. The path to the necropolis was empty, and they found no one among the graves. In the far corner was an old sarcophagus made of local stone. Resting on a slanted base, the stone box was chipped on one corner, and the lid was partially open. A garland had been engraved on the side, but most of its shape had long since faded. They moved toward the sarcophagus without a word. Virgos stepped up onto the base and turned around. She climbed in, lifted Batos' torso off of Virgos' back and laid him down carefully inside. She folded his arms in toward his chest, just as she had done in the play the night before. Virgos watched her say goodbye to him and then climb out. He noticed every movement and every step. It was an awkward choreography that could not be avoided or delegated. This was a painful and horrible love, but love all the more because of it.

They slid the stone lid until it reached the far end of the box and took a step back. Standing next to one another, Virgos searched for words in silence. The verses that came so easily in the play were disjointed and far from one another now. Kaineus started searching the ground for something. Unsure of what she was doing, he waited for her to explain. She placed several stones on top of the stone lid and shaped them in the form of a Greek letter *alpha*. With more stones, she made the word "*arete*." Inspired, Virgos collected stones and erected a small pillar on top of the lid next to the letters.

The voices of Isaiah and Daniel came to him. "Go through, go through," Virgos said. "Prepare the way. You shall rise for your reward at the end of days."

Chapter 32

Kaineus

A VOICE CALLED OUT from inside a stall. "He isn't here," the voice said. "Try the agora."

Kaineus and Virgos were searching for Ifran. The weight of the news they had to share slowed their pace. They walked slowly toward the main street of vendors. Both she and Virgos did not know what to say to Ifran, but they had to tell him what had happened. His friend, his brother, had been killed and was now lying in a stone box. The imperial temples and monuments of this city all looked the same to her: shallow, grandiose attempts to be recognized, praised, or remembered. Near the entrance to the south stoa, she noticed an inscription about the greatness of Gaius Caligula. It had been defaced. His name had been brought before a graffiti court and pronounced no longer worthy of memory.

"All is vanity," Virgos said as if he had understood her silent thoughts. "What do people gain from all their toil?" She touched his elbow out of gratitude. From a distance they spotted Ifran with a bowl of puls, smiling and talking with the woman who handed it to him. Kaineus started to raise her hand, and he raised his chin in acknowledgement. Turning away from the booth, he saw their faces and stood still. His smile faded as he studied them. It seemed as if he was speaking to them, but they could not hear him. He looked down at his feet and continued to speak as they approached.

When they reached him, he was speaking in the language that she remembered from their greeting the day before. They waited in silence until he was finished. He raised a hand and made the same gesture that Batos had made at the play. Three of his fingers pointed one direction, and two fingers folded under. Follow me, he seemed to say. The news of Batos' death had already been said.

Without a word, they followed him to the bouleterion. Open to the street, the seats were empty and gave them a place to sit together. Kaineus sat on one side of Ifran, and Virgos on the other. Ifran offered his food to each of them, and they shared it until the bowl was empty. He sat it on the seat behind him and stared at the horizon beyond the busy street. His mouth contorted, and he hung his head between his shoulders. Kaineus could think of nothing that would ease his grief. He raised his head and sucked a coriander seed out from behind his front teeth.

"Where did it happen?" he asked flatly.

"Down by the harbor," Virgos said.

"Are there any bodies?" he asked.

"One," Kaineus answered.

"And Batos? Where is he?"

"In an old sarcophagus near the outer edge of the necropolis," Kaineus said.

"I know the one. I will tend to him," Ifran answered. He adjusted his feet on the seat below him and brought them back to the same place they had been. "He couldn't ride a camel," he said, remembering with a subtle smile. 'We had to get out of Volubilis in a hurry. The Romans had taken all of our horses. Batos had trouble getting on the camel, and then when he did, the camel ran in the opposite direction. Straight back into the skirmish. He was bouncing around, hanging off either side, leaning forward and back." Ifran laughed quietly. "I went after him, running as fast as you can on a camel, and caught the reins. I said to Batos, 'Did you forget what side you were on?' We took off for the high country and got away. I don't know how we did. He was a natural horseman, but camels . . . " He shook his head and snorted air out of his nose. "I'll never forget that."

The images made Kaineus smile. One memory had become three. There was so much she did not know about Batos. It was as if Ifran had given her a cup of water from a well she would never visit again.

Ifran asked, "Are you on your way to Thessalonica? Batos said you were on a mission to find Paul of Tarsus." Both them agreed. "Do you want to take the horses?"

"No," she said. "They will be happiest here. We will go on foot."

"Take the animal trail north. It will be safer than the main road. Whoever followed you might have friends. When you get to the hot springs, you are almost to Troas. I'll show you where the trail starts. Come with me to the stable before you go. I can send some supplies with you." He paused. "I've never met Paul of Tarsus. Maybe someday he will come through here."

Kaineus liked the idea immediately. "Maybe we will be with him." She leaned around Ifran to speak to Virgos. "Didn't Aristotle live here? Didn't he write here, and start a school?"

"Yes to all," Virgos said thoughtfully.

"There is one particular work by Aristotle that I am thinking of. Something about virtue. I remember it being sung at a funeral once, when I was very young," she said.

"I have heard it," Virgos said, "though I remember only phrases. He wrote it in honor of his friend Hermias, who had died."

"We could write our own about Batos," Kaineus said.

Virgos began. "Virtue, who brings care and toil, yet you are life's best."

"To die is delicate," Kaineus continued, "to endure the pain, the stern strong ache."

"Fruit for our souls' comfort." Virgos alternated his verses with hers.

"Undying joy, more dear than gold."

"Immortal praise shall be his guardian."

"His goodness and his deeds are the burden of songs."

"Sung by Memory's daughters three."

"And friendship firm," Ifran added, speaking for the first time. He stood and stepped onto the ground. "Come with me. I will show you the path to Troas."

Chapter 33

Virgos

GIVEN THE EVENTS OF the last few days, Virgos had hoped to devote time to thought and prayer. Batos' death remained at a distance, an event that had happened to others on the horizon. The sharp jab of grief was inevitable, but for now, practical matters took precedence. He was attempting to keep up with Kaineus on the trail. She was walking as if she were on fire. He had not seen a human footprint, and most of the prints were of small hooves. It offered him a wide panoramic view, occasionally obscured by shrubs, but often open to the sea.

He called up and named the memories of each day of the journey he had undertaken with Kaineus, Batos, Leah, Myrina, and then Ifran. Like a poem, each day had stanzas that he tried to commit to memory. He did not want to lose one image or one word. Unlike the wandering Hebrews, he was not carrying a prophet's bones. Batos would remain in Assos with his friend and their shared story.

Virgos adjusted the scroll case strap and searched the trail ahead for sign of Kaineus. She was so far ahead that he did not see her. Behind him, he heard a rhythmic series of sounds. Cupping and knocking sounds that were not human. He stopped and stepped off the trail to look behind him. Walking toward him on the dust was a small, single-minded donkey. Moving quickly, with a small swing of the head at each step, the donkey did not look up or acknowledge his presence in any way. Virgos sped up to walk by the donkey's side, but still the donkey did not look up.

"Are you going to Jerusalem, too?" Virgos asked. He expected the donkey to say something in response, but he did not know why. As they reached a fork in the trail, Virgos stopped. On his own mission, the donkey turned to the left and walked down the hill. Virgos stood at the crossroads and watched the donkey until he was out of sight.

Kaineus' voice turned his head to the right. "I found the hot springs!" she said with excitement from the top of the dune. "And I can see Troas!"

"Coming, dear Jael," he said. His words were part speech, part song. He followed her footprints as topped the dune and saw Kaineus waiting for him.

Tucked into a circle of pines, the thermal spring welled up from the ground at the end of a small stream. Kaineus slid in fully clothed. Virgos lifted the scroll case over his head and carefully laid it off to the side. He slid in beside her and felt the water seep through his clothes. Aching from the long walk, he laid his head back onto a tuft of squill that had not yet bloomed. He swirled his hand over the surface of the water and saw a small newt floating next to him. It reminded him of a nymph he had seen in a mosaic.

"What are we doing, Virgos?" Kaineus asked. "I don't know who Paul is. I don't know who Jesus is."

"Paul is a mystery," Virgos said. "But Jesus is starting to take shape. He went ahead of us, past the frontier and into death. He came back for us. He is here now, at the edges of things, in the spaces between. All the world is holy and loved. Loved beyond measure."

"A forerunner of love," Kaineus said quietly. "Lead on."

Chapter 34

Kaineus

THE TRAVELERS KNELT NEAR a large marble head of Dionysus and studied the items they had stolen: a sistrum, a pomegranate, a pine bough, a small votive statue of a mouse, and a bucket of blood from the butcher. "What shall we do?" Virgos mused. "What disguise can we assemble from this fine collection?"

Now that they had reached Troas, their thoughts turned to the instructions they had received. By example if not by word, Batos had taught them to stay awake and be vigilant. Ifran had warned of others who might be following them. Leah had told them of a stone merchant ship that would give them safe transport. They may have to take multiple boats to Thessalonica, but the stone merchant would take them as far as he could. As far as Kaineus knew, they had not been followed, and the colony of soldiers in Troas posed no obstacles for them. Dim-witted, insular, and oblivious, she thought, as she and Virgos walked by their street game of knuckle bones. Batos would not have dismissed them as a potential threat, but he could have easily outsmarted them. He had a keen eye and a quiet confidence that inspired her. It did not seem possible that he was gone. She could still hear his voice.

Kaineus opened her travel bag and pulled out the crown from the first play in Pergamum, and the saffron veil she wore at her husband's funeral. "Add these to the pile," she said, arranging them on the ground in front of them.

"Let's confuse them," Virgos said.

"Yes! Wait. What?" Kaineus asked quizzically.

"Let's mix up gods, symbols, languages, kings. Let's mix it up. Let's be as confusing and disturbing as possible."

Kaineus was ready for the ruse, but had one question. "What would that look like?

"We will improvise," Virgos said, recalling their apocalypse in Assos. "We can make it up together."

"Let's do it," Kaineus said. She wrapped the veil around her head and put the crown on top. She grasped the pomegranate with one hand and the mouse votive in the other. Virgos picked up the sistrum and pine bough and then put them down again.

"That leaves the blood," he said, furrowing his brow. "Oh! I know." He picked up the bucket and dumped blood on his groin.

Kaineus shot him a reproving look. "Do you have to do that?" she said.

He shrugged with one shoulder and grinned. "Let them wonder," he said. She sighed and shook her head. He picked up the pine bough and sistrum and said, "Let's go!"

Shaking the sistrum with one hand and swirling the pine bough in the air with the other, Virgos skipped down the center of the agora toward the harbor. "Has anyone seen Cybele?" he asked bystanders. "She did not come when we called her. Cybele, where are you?" Kaineus followed close behind, singing loudly of the destruction of Babylon in Latin. Virgos joined in the song and added a verse about the Red Sea. She could sense the judgment and disapproval of the crowds as they made their way through the streets. She was not afraid of their looks and whispers. She relished the raucous scene and began to feel the freedom she sought back in Pergamum.

When they reached the harbor, they saw a man loading pieces of fine marble into a boat. Virgos approached him and said, "We are on a sacred journey. We have a message for King Nebuchadnezzar. Could you transport us to Thessalonica?"

The man put down a chunk of marble and turned to face them. "The King is expecting us," Kaineus said. "We have been travelling for so long. Did we miss Lupercalia?"

"Lupercalia was months ago," Virgos said, patting her shoulder. "Do not be afraid, Nana. Just hold on to your pomegranate and mouse. We will arrive at the appointed time."

She gripped her props tightly and smiled as if she were dizzy. "The Day of Joy is here at last! We approach the inner chamber!" she shouted.

"Are you actors?" the merchant asked.

Virgos responded with open arms. "Are we not all actors in the Great Drama? Do we not all play a role of the utmost importance?"

"Leah's people?" the merchant asked, although it seemed he knew the answer to his question.

"Leah!" Kaineus said. "A fern grows in the wilderness and provides shade for the weary. The prophet has foretold. Are you the one who will show us the way?"

The merchant gestured toward the bow of the boat. "Climb in," he said. "I will take you as far as I can."

Virgos smiled at her and stepped into the shallow water near the bow. He stopped suddenly and leaned over to pick something up. Kaineus could not see what he was reaching for until he stood up. He was holding a frog in the palm of his hand. He spoke to the frog in Hebrew and gently set the frog down in the sand. She heard the stone merchant laugh softly.

"What did you say?" she asked.

"Be fruitful and multiply, but not too much," Virgos translated.

"Will you teach me Hebrew?" she asked Virgos as they settled into the boat.

"Yes," he said. "We have time."

She felt a gust of wind on her brow. It cooled the sweat that had formed there. "Thank you, Lord Jesus," the merchant said as he pulled up the anchor and watched the sail burst open. Kaineus remembered the group refrain in Leah's house. He must be one of her people, too.

She turned to Virgos, who was smiling broadly. They had the same thought at the same instant. "Thank you, Lord Jesus," they said in unison to one another. She did not know what would happen in the coming days. She did not know if Paul was still in Thessalonica, or if he would help them understand who Jesus was. But she was certain that the way had unfolded before them as if it had been prepared for them. Each leg of the journey had been guided by hands seen and unseen. She looked up at the full sail and then out at the horizon. The wind would carry them where they needed to be.

The End